PHILIP STEELE

OF THE ROYAL NORTHWEST
MOUNTED POLICE

James Oliver Curwood

1ˢᵗ WORLD
LIBRARY
Literary Society

Philip Steele of the Royal Northwest Mounted Police

James Oliver Curwood

© 1st World Library – Literary Society, 2006
PO Box 2211
Fairfield, IA 52556
www.1stworldlibrary.org
First Edition

LCCN: 2006905717

Softcover ISBN: 1-4218-2146-X
Hardcover ISBN: 1-4218-2046-3
eBook ISBN: 1-4218-2246-6

Purchase *"Philip Steele of the Royal Northwest Mounted Police"*
as a traditional bound book at:
www.1stWorldLibrary.org/purchase.asp?ISBN=1-4218-2146-X

1st World Library Literary Society is a nonprofit
organization dedicated to promoting literacy by:

- Creating a free internet library accessible from any
computer worldwide.
- Hosting writing competitions and offering book
publishing scholarships.

**Readers interested in supporting literacy
through sponsorship, donations or
membership please contact:
literacy@1stworldlibrary.org
Check us out at: www.1stworldlibrary.ORG
and start downloading free ebooks today.**

Philip Steele of the Royal Northwest Mounted Police
contributed by Tim, Ed & Rodney
in support of
1st World Library Literary Society

CHAPTER I

THE HYACINTH LETTER

Philip Steele's pencil drove steadily over the paper, as if the mere writing of a letter he might never mail in some way lessened the loneliness.

The wind is blowing a furious gale outside. From off the lake come volleys of sleet, like shot from guns, and all the wild demons of this black night in the wilderness seem bent on tearing apart the huge end-locked logs that form my cabin home. In truth, it is a terrible night to be afar from human companionship, with naught but this roaring desolation about and the air above filled with screeching terrors. Even through thick log walls I can hear the surf roaring among the rocks and beating the white driftwood like a thousand battering-rams, almost at my door. It is a night to make one shiver, and in the lulls of the storm the tall pines above me whistle and wail mournfully as they straighten their twisted heads after the blasts.

To-morrow this will be a desolation of snow. There will be snow from here to Hudson's Bay, from the Bay to the Arctic, and where now there is all this fury and strife of wind and sleet there will be unending quiet - the stillness which breeds our tongueless people of the North. But this is small comfort for tonight. Yesterday I caught a little mouse in my flour and killed him. I am sorry now, for surely all this trouble and thunder in the night would have driven him out from his home in the wall to keep me company.

It would not be so bad if it were not for the skull. Three times in the last half-hour I have started to take it down from its shelf over my crude stone fireplace, where pine logs are blazing. But each time I have fallen back, shivering, into the bed-like chair I have made for myself out of saplings and caribou skin. It is a human skull. Only a short time ago it was a living man, with a voice, and eyes, and brain - and that is what makes me uncomfortable. If it were an old skull, it would be different. But it is a new skull. Almost I fancy at times that there is life lurking in the eyeless sockets, where the red firelight from the pitch-weighted logs plays in grewsome flashes; and I fancy, too, that in the brainless cavities of the skull there must still be some of the old passion, stirred into spirit life by the very madness of this night. A hundred times I have been sorry that I kept the thing, but never more so than now.

How the wind howls and the pines screech above me! A pailful of snow, plunging down my chimney, sends the chills up my spine as if it were the very devil himself, and the steam of it surges out and upward and hides the skull. It is absurd to go to bed, to make an effort to sleep, for I know what my dreams would be. To-night they would be filled with this skull - and with visions of a face, a woman's face -

Thus far had Steele written, when with a nervous laugh he sprang from his chair, and with something that sounded very near to an oath, in the wild tumult of the storm, crumpled the paper in his hand and flung it among the blazing logs he had described but a few moments before.

"Confound it, this will never do!" he exclaimed, falling into his own peculiar habit of communing with himself. "I say it won't do, Phil Steele; deuce take it if it will! You're getting nervous, sentimental, almost homesick. Ugh, what a beast of a night!"

He turned to the rude stone fireplace again as another blast of

James Oliver Curwood

snow plunged down the chimney.

"Wish I'd built a fire in the stove instead of there," he went on, filling his pipe. "Thought it would be a little more cheerful, you know. Lord preserve us, listen to that!"

He began walking up and down the hewn log floor of the cabin, his hands deep in his pockets, puffing out voluminous clouds of smoke. It was not often that Philip Steele's face was unpleasant to look upon, but to-night it wore anything but its natural good humor. It was a strong, thin face, set off by a square jaw, and with clear, steel-gray eyes in which just now there shone a strange glitter, as they rested for a moment upon the white skull over the fire. From his scrutiny of the skull Steele turned to a rough board table, lighted by a twisted bit of cotton cloth, three-quarters submerged in a shallow tin of caribou grease. In the dim light of this improvised lamp there were two letters, opened and soiled, which an Indian had brought up to him from Nelson House the day before. One of them was short and to the point. It was an official note from headquarters ordering him to join a certain Buck Nome at Lac Bain, a hundred miles farther north.

It was the second letter which Steele took in his hands for the twentieth time since it had come to him here, three hundred miles into the wilderness. There were half-a-dozen pages of it, written in a woman's hand, and from it there rose to his nostrils the faint, sweet perfume of hyacinth. It was this odor that troubled him - that had troubled him since yesterday, and that made him restless and almost homesick to-night. It took him back to things - to the days of not so very long ago when he had been a part of the life from which the letter came, and when the world had seemed to hold for him all that one could wish. In a retrospective flash there passed before him a vision of those days, when he, Mr. Philip Steele, son of a multimillionaire banker, was one of the favored few in the social life of a great city; when fashionable clubs opened their doors to him, and beautiful women smiled upon him, and when, among others, this girl of the hyacinth letter held out to him the tempting lure of her heart. Her heart? Or was it the tempting of his own wealth? Steele laughed, and his strong white teeth gleamed in a half-contemptuous smile as he turned again toward the fire.

He sat down, with the letter still in his hands, and thought of some of those others whom he had known. What had become of Jack Moody, he wondered - the good old Jack of his college days, who had loved this girl of the hyacinth with the whole of his big, honest heart, but who hadn't been given half a show because of his poverty? And where was Whittemore, the young broker whose hopes had fallen with his own financial ruin; and Fordney, who would have cut off ten years of his life for her - and half-a-dozen others he might name?

Her heart! Steele laughed softly as he lifted the letter so that the sweet perfume of it came to him more strongly. How she had tempted him for a time! Almost - that night of the Hawkins' ball - he had surrendered to her. He half-closed his eyes, and as the logs crackled in the fireplace and the wind roared outside, he saw her again as he had seen her that night - gloriously beautiful; memory of the witchery of her voice, her hair, her eyes firing his blood like strong wine. And this beauty might have been for him, was still his, if he chose. A word from out of the wilderness, a few lines that he might write to-night -

With a sudden jerk Steele sat bolt upright. One after another he crumpled the sheets of paper in his hand and tossed all but the signature page into the fire. The last sheet he kept, studied it for a little - as if her name were the answer to a problem - then laid it aside. For a few moments there remained still the haunting sweetness of the hyacinth. When it was gone, he gave a last searching sniff, rose to his feet with a laugh in which there was some return of his old spirit, hid that final page of her letter in his traveling kit and proceeded to refill his pipe.

More than once Philip Steele had told himself that he was born a century or two after his time. He had admitted this

James Oliver Curwood

much to a few of his friends, and they had laughed at him. One evening he had opened his heart a little to the girl of the hyacinth letter, and after that she had called him eccentric. Within himself he knew that he was unlike other men, that the blood in him was calling back to almost forgotten generations, when strong hearts and steady hands counted for manhood rather than stocks and bonds, and when romance and adventure were not quite dead. At college he took civil engineering, because it seemed to him to breathe the spirit of outdoors; and when he had finished he incurred the wrath of those at home by burying himself for a whole year with a surveying expedition in Central America.

It was this expedition that put the finishing touch to Philip Steele. He came back a big hearted, clear minded young fellow, as bronzed as an Aztec - a hater of cities and the hothouse varieties of pleasure to which he had been born, and as far removed from anticipation of his father's millions as though they had never been. He possessed a fortune in his own right, but as yet he had found no use for the income that was piling up. A second expedition, this time to Brazil, and then he came back - to meet the girl of the hyacinth letter. And after that, after he had broken from the bondage which held Moody, and Fordney, and Whittemore, he went back to his many adventures.

It was the North that held him. In the unending desolations of snow and forest and plain, between Hudson's Bay and the wild country of the Athabasca, he found the few people and the mystery and romance which carried him back, and linked him to the dust-covered generations he had lost. One day a slender, athletically built young man enlisted at Regina for service in the Northwest Mounted Police. Within six months he had made several records for himself, and succeeded in having himself detailed to service in the extreme North, where man-hunting became the thrilling game of One against One in an empty and voiceless world. And no one, not even the girl of the hyacinth letter, would have dreamed that the man who was officially listed as "Private Phil Steele, of the N.W.M.P.," was

Philip Steele, millionaire and gentleman adventurer.

None appreciated the humor of this fact more than Steele himself, and he fell again into his wholesome laugh as he placed a fresh pine log on the fire, wondering what his aristocratic friends - and especially the girl of the hyacinth letter - would say if they could see him and his environment just at the present moment. In a slow, chuckling survey he took in the heavy German socks which he had hung to dry close to the fire; his worn shoe-packs, shining in a thick coat of caribou grease, and his single suit of steaming underwear that he had washed after supper, and which hung suspended from the ceiling, looking for all the world, in the half dusk of the cabin, like a very thin and headless man. In this gloom, indeed, but one thing shone out white and distinct - the skull on the little shelf above the fire. As his eyes rested on it, Steele's lips tightened and his face grew dark. With a sudden movement he reached up and took it in his hands, holding it for a moment so that the light from the fire flashed full upon it. In the left side, on a line with the eyeless socket and above the ear, was a hole as large as a small egg.

"So I'm ordered up to join Nome, the man who did this, eh?" he muttered, fingering the ragged edge. "I could kill him for what happened down there at Nelson House, M'sieur Janette. Some day - I may."

He balanced the skull on his finger tips, level with his chin.

"Nice sort of a chap for a Hamlet, I am," he went on, whimsically. "I believe I'll chuck you into the fire, M'sieur Janette. You're getting on my nerves."

He stopped suddenly and lowered the skull to the table.

"No, I won't burn you," he continued, "I've brought you this far and I'll pack you up to Lac Bain with me. Some morning I'll give you to Bucky Nome for breakfast. And then, M'sieur - then we shall see what we shall see."

Later that night he wrote a few words on a slip of paper and tacked the paper to the inside of his door. To any who might follow in his footsteps it conveyed this information and advice:

NOTICE!

This cabin and what's in it are quasheed by me. Fill your gizzard but not your pockets.

Steele, Northwest Mounted.

CHAPTER II

A FACE OUT OF THE NIGHT

Steele came up to the Hudson's Bay Company's post at Lac Bain on the seventh day after the big storm, and Breed, the factor, confided two important bits of information to him while he was thawing out before the big box-stove in the company's deserted and supply-stripped store. The first was that a certain Colonel Becker and his wife had left Fort Churchill, on Hudson's Bay, to make a visit at Lac Bain; the second, that Buck Nome had gone westward a week before and had not returned. Breed was worried, not over Nome's prolonged absence, but over the anticipated arrival of the other two. According to the letter which had come to him from the Churchill factor. Colonel Becker and his wife had come over on the last supply ship from London, and the colonel was a high official in the company's service. Also, he was an old gentleman. Ostensibly he had no business at Lac Bain, but was merely on a vacation, and wished to see a bit of real life in the wilderness.

Breed's grizzled face was miserable.

"Why don't they send 'em down to York Factory or Nelson House?" he demanded of Steele. "They've got duck feathers, three women, and a civilized factor at the Nelson, and there ain't any of 'em here - not even a woman!"

Steele shrugged his shoulders as Breed mentioned the three

women at Nelson.

"There are only two women there now," he replied. "Since a certain Bucky Nome passed that way, one of them has gone into the South."

"Well, two, then," said Breed, who had not caught the flash of fire in the other's eyes. "But I tell you there ain't a one here, Steele, not even an Indian - and that dirty Cree, Jack, is doing the cooking. Blessed Saints, I caught him mixing biscuit dough in the wash basin the other day, and I've been eating those biscuits ever since our people went out to their traplines! There's you, and Nome, two Crees, a 'half' and myself - and that's every soul there'll be at Lac Bain until the mid-winter run of fur. Now, what in Heaven's name is the poor old Mrs. Colonel going to do?"

"Got a bed for her?"

"A bunk - hard as nails!"

"Good grub?"

"Rotten!" groaned the factor. "Every trapper's son of them took out big supplies this fall and we're stripped. Beans, flour, sugar'n'prunes - and caribou until I feel like turning inside out every time I smell it. I'd give a month's commission for a pound of pork. Look here! If this letter ain't 'quality' you can cut me into jiggers. Bet the Mrs. Colonel wrote it for her hubby."

From an inside pocket Breed drew forth a square white envelope with a broken seal of red wax, and from it extracted a folded sheet of cream-tinted paper. Scarcely had Steele taken the note in his hands when a quick thrill passed through him. Before he had read the first line he was conscious again of that haunting sweetness in the air he breathed - the perfume of hyacinth. There was not only this perfume, but the same paper, the same delicately pretty writing of the letter he had burned more than a week before. He made no effort to suppress the exclamation of astonishment that broke from his lips. Breed was staring at him when he lifted his eyes.

"This is a mighty strange coincidence, Breed," he said, regaining his composure. "I could almost swear that I know this writing, and yet of course such a thing is impossible. Still, it's mighty queer. Will you let me keep the letter until tonight? I'd like to take it over to the cabin and compare it -"

"Needn't return it at all," interrupted the factor. "Hope you find something interesting to tell me at supper - five sharp. It will be a blessing if you know 'em."

Ten minutes later Steele was in the little cabin which he and Nome occupied while at Lac Bain. Jack, the Cree, had built a rousing fire in the long sheet-iron stove, and as Steele opened its furnace-like door, a flood of light poured out into the gathering gloom of early evening. Drawing a chair full into the light, he again opened the letter. Line for line and word for word he scrutinized the writing, and with each breath that he drew he found himself more deeply thrilled by a curious mental excitement which it was impossible for him to explain. According to the letter. Colonel and Mrs. Becker had arrived at Churchill aboard the London ship a little over a month previously. He remembered that the date on the letter from the girl was six weeks old. At the time it was written, Colonel Becker and his wife were either in London or Liverpool, or crossing the Atlantic. No matter how similar the two letters appeared to him, he realized that, under the circumstances, the same person could not have written them both. For many minutes he sat back in his chair, with his eyes half-closed, absorbing the comforting heat of the fire. Again the old vision returned to him. In a subconscious sort of way he found himself fighting against it, as he had struggled a score of times to throw off its presence, since the girl's letter had come to him. And this time, as before, his effort was futile. He saw her again - and always as on that night of the Hawkins' ball, eyes and lips smiling at him, the light shining gloriously in the deep red gold of her hair.

With an effort Steele aroused himself and looked at his watch. It was a quarter of five. He stooped to close the stove door, and stopped suddenly, his hand reaching out, head and shoulders hunched over. Across his knee, shining in the firelight, like a thread of spun gold, lay a single filament of a woman's hair.

He rose slowly, holding the hair between him and the light. His fingers trembled, his breath came quickly. The hair had fallen upon his knee from the letter - or the envelope, and it was wonderfully like HER hair!

From the direction of the factor's quarters came the deep bellowing of Breed's moose-horn, calling him to supper. Before he responded to it, Steele wound the silken thread of gold about his ringer, then placed it carefully among the papers and cards which he carried in his leather wallet. His face was flushed when he joined the factor. Not since the night at the Hawkins' ball, when he had felt the touch of a beautiful woman's hands, the warmth of her breath, the soft sweep of her hair against his lips as he had leaned over her in his half-surrender, had thought of woman stirred him as he felt himself stirred now. He was glad that Breed was too much absorbed in his own troubles to observe any possible change in himself or to ask questions about the letter.

"I tell you, it may mean the short birch for me, Steele," said the factor gloomily. "Lac Bain is just now the emptiest, most fallen-to-pieces, unbusiness-like post between the Athabasca and the Bay. We've had two bad seasons running, and every-thing has gone wrong. Colonel Becker is a big one with the company. Ain't no doubt about that, and ten to one he'll think it's a new man that's wanted here."

"Nonsense!" exclaimed Steele. A sudden flash shot into his face as he looked hard at Breed. "See here, how would you like to have me go out to meet them?" he asked. "Sort of a welcoming committee of one, you know. Before they got here I could casually give 'em to understand what Lac Bain has been up against during the last two seasons."

Breed's face brightened in an instant.

"That might save us, Steele. Will you do it?"

"With pleasure."

Philip was conscious of an increasing warmth in his face as he bent over his plate. "You're sure - they're elderly people?" he asked.

"That is what MacVeigh wrote me from Churchill; at least he said the colonel was an old man."

"And his wife?"

"Has got her nerve," growled Breed irreverently. "It wouldn't be so bad if it was only the colonel. But an old woman - ugh! What he doesn't think of she'll remind him of, you can depend on that."

Steele thought of his mother, who looked at things through a magnifying lorgnette, and laughed a little cheerlessly.

"I'll go out and meet them, anyway," he comforted. "Have Jack fix me up for the hike in the morning, Breed. I'll start after breakfast."

He was glad when supper was over and he was back in his own cabin smoking his pipe. It was almost with a feeling of shame that he took the golden hair from his wallet and held it once more so that it shone before his eyes in the firelight.

"You're crazy, Phil Steele," he assured himself. "You're an unalloyed idiot. What the deuce has Colonel Becker's wife got to do with you - even if she has golden hair and uses cream-tinted paper soaked in hyacinth? Confound it - there!" and he released the shining hair from his fingers so that the air currents sent it floating back into the deeper gloom of the cabin.

It was midnight before he went to bed. He was up with the first cold gray of dawn. All that day he strode steadily eastward on snowshoes, over the company's trail to the bay. Two hours before dusk he put up his light tent, gathered balsam for a bed, and built a fire of dry spruce against the face of a huge rock in front of his shelter. It was still light when he wrapped himself in his blanket and lay down on the balsam, with his feet stretched out to the reflected heat of the big rock. It seemed to Steele that there was an unnatural stillness in the air, as the night thickened beyond the rim of firelight, and, as the gloom grew still deeper, blotting out his vision in inky blackness, there crept over him slowly a feeling of loneliness. It was a new sensation to Steele, and he shivered as he sat up and faced the fire. It was this same quiet, this same unending mystery of voiceless desolation that had won him to the North. Until to-night he had loved it. But now there was something oppressive about it, something that made him strain his eyes to see beyond the rock and the fire, and set his ears in tense listening for sounds which did not exist. He knew that in this hour he was longing for companionship - not that of Breed, nor of men with whom he hunted men, but of men and women whom he had once known and in whose lives he had played a part - ages ago, it seemed to him. He knew, as he sat with clenched hands and staring eyes, that chiefly he was longing for a woman - a woman whose eyes and lips and sunny hair haunted him after months of forgetfulness, and whose face smiled at him luringly, now, from out the leaping flashes of fire - tempting him, calling him over a thousand miles of space. And if he yielded -

The thought sent his nails biting into the flesh of his palms and he sank back with a curse that held more of misery than blasphemy. Physical exhaustion rather than desire for sleep closed his eyes, at last, in half-slumber, and after that the face seemed nearer and more real to him, until it was close at his side, and was speaking to him. He heard again the soft, rippling laugh, girlishly sweet, that had fascinated him at Hawkins' ball; he heard the distant hum and chatter of other voices, and then one loud and close - that of Chesbro, who had unwittingly interrupted them, and saved him, just in the nick of time.

Steele moved restlessly; after a moment wriggled to his elbow and looked toward the fire. He seemed to hear Chesbro's voice again as he awoke, and a thrill as keen as an electric shock set his nerves tingling when he heard once more the laughing voice of his dream, hushed and low. In amazement he sat bolt upright and stared. Was he still dreaming? The fire was burning brightly and he was aware that he had scarce fallen into sleep.

A movement - a sound of feet crunching softly in the snow, and a figure came between him and the fire.

It was a woman.

He choked back the cry that rose to his lips and sat motionless and without sound. The figure approached a step nearer, peering into the deep gloom of the tent. He caught the silver glint in the firelight on heavy fur, the whiteness of a hand touching lightly the flap of his tent, and then for an instant he saw a face. In that instant he sat as rigid as if he had stopped the beat of his own life. A pair of dark eyes laughing in at him, a flash of laughing teeth, a low titter that was scarce more than a rippling throat-note, and the face was gone, leaving him still staring into the blank space where it had been.

With a cough to give warning of his wakefulness, Steele flung off his blanket and drew himself through the low opening of the tent. On the extreme right of the fire stood a man and woman, warming themselves over the coals. They straightened from their leaning posture as he appeared.

"This is too bad, too bad, Mr. Steele," exclaimed the man,

James Oliver Curwood

advancing quickly. "I was afraid we'd make a blunder and awaken you. We were about to camp on a mountain back there when we saw your fire and drove on to it. I'm sorry -"

"Wouldn't have had you miss me for anything," interrupted Steele, gripping the other's proffered hand. "You see, I'm out from Lac Bain to meet Colonel and Mrs. Becker, and - " He hesitated purposely, his white teeth gleaming in the frank smile which made people like him immensely, from the first.

"You've met them," completed the laughing voice from across the fire. "Please, Mr. Steele, will you forgive me for looking in at you and waking you up? But your feet looked so terribly funny, and I assure you that was all I could see, though I tried awfully hard. Anyway, I saw your name printed on the flap of your tent."

Steele felt a slow fire burning in his cheeks as he encountered the beautiful eyes glowing at him from behind the colonel. The woman was smiling at him. In the heat of the fire she had pushed back her fur turban, and he saw that her hair was the same shining red gold that had come to him in the letter, and that her lips and eyes and the glorious color in her face were remarkably like those of which he had dreamed, and of which waking visions had come with the hyacinth letter to fill him with unrest and homesickness. In spite of himself he had reasoned that she would be young and that she would have golden hair, but these other things, the laughing beauty of her face, the luring depth of her eyes.

He caught himself staring.

"I - I was dreaming," he almost stammered. He pulled himself together quickly. "I was dreaming of a face, Mrs. Becker, It seems strange that this should happen - away up here, in this way. The face that I dreamed of is a thousand miles from here, and it is wonderfully like yours."

The colonel was laughing at him when he turned. He was a

little man, as straight as a gun rod, pale of face except for his nose, which was nipped red by the cold, and with a pointed beard as white as the snow under his feet. That part of his countenance which exposed itself above the top of his great fur coat and below his thick beaver cap was alive with good cheer, notwithstanding its pallor.

"Glad you're good humored about it, Steele," he cried with an immediate tone of comradeship. "We wouldn't have ventured into your camp if it hadn't been for Isobel. She was positively insistent, sir. Wanted to see who was here and what it looked like. Eh, Isobel, my dear, are you satisfied?"

"I surely didn't expect to find 'It' asleep at this time of the day," said Mrs. Becker. She laughed straight into Philip's face, and so roguishly sweet was the curve of her red lips and the light in her eyes that his heart quickened its beating, and the flush deepened in his cheeks.

"It's only six," he said, looking at his watch. "I don't usually turn in this early. I was tired to-night - though I am not, now," he added quickly. "I could sit up until morning - and talk. We don't often meet people from outside, you know. Where are the others?"

"Back there," said the colonel, waving an arm into the gloom. "Isobel made 'em sit down and be quiet, dogs and all, sir, while we came on alone. There are Indians, two sledges, and a ton of duff."

"Call them," said Steele. "There's room for your tent beside mine, Colonel, close against the face of this rock. It's as good as a furnace."

The colonel moved a little out into the gloom and shouted to those behind. Philip turned to find Mrs. Becker looking at him in a timid, questioning sort of way, the laughter gone from her eyes. For a moment she seemed to be on the point of speaking to him, then picked up a short stick and began toying with the coals.

"You must be tired, Mrs. Becker," he said. "Now that you are near a fire, I would suggest that you throw off your heavy coat. You will be more comfortable, and I will bring you a blanket to sit on."

He dived into his tent and a moment later reappeared with a blanket, which he spread close against the butt of a big spruce within half a dozen feet of the fire. When he turned toward her, the colonel's wife had thrown off her coat and turban and stood before him, a slim and girlish figure, bewitchingly pretty as she smiled her gratitude and nestled down into the place he had prepared for her. For a moment he bent over her, tucking the thick fur about her feet and knees, and in that moment he breathed from the heavy coils of her shining hair the flower-like sweetness which had already stirred him to the depths of his soul.

Colonel Becker was smiling down upon them when he straightened up, and at the humorous twinkle in his eyes, as he gazed from one to the other, Steele felt that the guilt of his own thoughts was blazing in his face. He was glad that the Indians came up with the sledges just at this moment, and as he went back to help them with the dogs and packs he swore softly at himself for the heat that was in his blood and the strange madness that was firing his brain. And inwardly he cursed himself still more when he returned to the fire. From out the deep gloom he saw the colonel sitting with his back against the spruce and Mrs. Becker nestling against him, her head resting upon his shoulder, talking and laughing up into his face. Even as he hesitated for an instant, scarce daring to break upon the scene, he saw her pull the gray-bearded face down to hers and kiss it, and in the ineffable contentment and happiness shining in the two faces in the firelight Philip Steele knew that he was looking upon that which had broken for ever the haunting image of another woman in his heart. In its place would remain this picture of love - love as he had dreamed of it, as he had hoped for it, and which he had found at last - but not for himself - in the heart of a wilderness.

He saw now something childishly sweet and pure in the face that smiled welcome to him as he came noisily through the snow-crust; and something, too, in the colonel's face, which reached out and gripped at his very heartstrings, and filled him with a warm glow that was new and strange to him, and which was almost the happiness of these two. It swept from him the sense of loneliness which had oppressed him a short time before, and when at last, after they had talked for a long time beside the fire, the colonel's wife lifted her pretty head drowsily and asked if she might go to bed, he laughed in sheer joy at the pouting tenderness with which she rubbed her pink cheek against the grizzled face above her, and at the gentle light in the colonel's eyes as he half carried her into the tent.

For a long time after he had rolled himself in his own blanket Philip lay awake, wondering at the strangeness of this thing that had happened to him. It was Her hair that he had seen shining this night under the old spruce, lustrous and soft, and coiled in its simple glory, as he had seen it last on the night when Chesbro had broken in on them at the ball. It was very easy for him to imagine that it had been Her face, with soul and heart and love added to its beauty. More than ever he knew what had been missing for him now, and blessed Chesbro for his blundering, and fell asleep to dream of the new face, and to awaken hours later to the unpleasant realization that his visions were but dream-fabric after all, and that the woman was the wife of Colonel Becker.

James Oliver Curwood

CHAPTER III

A SKULL AND A FLIRTATION

It was late afternoon when they came into Lac Bain, and as soon as Philip had turned over the colonel and his wife to Breed, he hurried to his own cabin. At the door he encountered Buck Nome. The two men had not met since a month before at Nelson House, and there was but little cordiality in Sng to say howdy to 'em," explained Nome, pausing for a moment. "Deuce of a good joke on you, Steele! How do you like the job of bringing in an old colonel's frozen wife, or a frozen colonel's old wife, eh?"

Every fiber in Steele's body grew tense at the banter in the other's voice. He whirled upon Nome, who had partly turned away.

"You remember - you lied down there at Nelson to get just such a 'job' as this," he reminded. "Have you forgotten what happened - after that?"

"Don't get miffed about it, man," returned Nome with an irritating laugh. "All's fair in love and war. That was love down there, 'pon my word of honor it was, and this is about as near the other thing as I want to come."

There was something in his laugh that drew Steele's lips in a tight line as he entered the cabin. It was not the first time that he had listened to Nome's gloating chuckle at the mention of certain women. It was this more than anything else that made him hate the man.

Physically, Nome was a magnificent specimen, beyond doubt the handsomest man in the service north of Winnipeg; so that while other men despised him for what they knew, women admired and loved him - until, now and then too late for their own salvation, they discovered that his moral code was rotten to the core.

Such a thing had happened at Nelson House, and Philip felt himself burning with a desire to choke the life out of Nome as he recalled the tragedy there. And what would happen - now? The thought came to him like a dash of cold water, and yet, after a moment, his teeth gleamed in a smile as a vision rose before him of the love and purity which he had seen in the sweet face of the colonel's wife. He chuckled softly to himself as he dragged out a pack from under his bunk; but there was no humor in the chuckle. From it he took a bundle wrapped in soft birch-bark, and from this produced the skull that he had brought up with him from the South. There was a tremble of excitement in his low laugh as he glanced about the gloomy interior of the cabin.

From the log ceiling hung a big oil lamp with a tin reflector, and under this he hung the skull.

"You'll make a pretty ornament, M'sieur Janette," he exclaimed, standing off to contemplate the white thing leering and bobbing at him from the end of its string. "Mon Dieu, I tell you that when the lamp is lighted Bucky Nome must be blind if he doesn't recognize you, even though you're dead, M'sieur!"

He lighted a smaller lamp, shaved himself, and changed his clothes. It was dark when he was ready for supper, and Nome had not returned. He waited a quarter of an hour longer, then put on his cap and coat and lighted the big oil lamp. At the door he turned to look back. The cavernous sockets of the skull stared at him. From where he stood he could see the ragged hole above the ear.

"It's your game to-night, M'sieur Janette," he cried back softly, and closed the door behind him.

They were gathered before a huge fire of logs in the factor's big living-room when Philip joined the others. A glance told him why Nome had not returned to the cabin. Breed and the colonel were smoking cigars over a ragged ledger of stupendous size, which the factor had spread out upon a small table, and both were deeply absorbed. Mrs. Becker was facing the fire, and close beside her sat Nome, leaning toward her and talking in a voice so low that only a murmur of it came to Steele's ears. The man's face was flushed when he looked up, and his eyes shone with the old fire which made Philip hate him.

As the woman turned to greet him Steele felt a suddenly sickening sensation grip at his heart. Her cheeks, too, were flushed, and the color in them deepened still more when he bowed to her and joined the two men at the table. The colonel shook hands with him, and Philip noticed that once or twice after that his eyes shifted uneasily in the direction of the two before the fire, and that whenever the low laughter of Mrs. Becker and Nome came to them he paid less attention to the columns of figures which Breed was pointing out to him. When they rose to go into supper, Philip's blood boiled as Nome offered his arm to Mrs. Becker, who accepted it with a swift, laughing glance at the colonel. There was no response in the older man's pale face, and Philip's fingers dug hard into the palms of his hands. At the table Nome's attentions to Mrs. Becker were even more marked. Once, under pretext of helping her to a dish, he whispered words which brought a deeper flush to her cheeks, and when she looked at the colonel his eyes were fixed upon her in stern reproof. It was abominable! Was Nome mad? Was the woman -

Steele did not finish the thought in his own mind. His eyes encountered those of the colonel's wife across the table. He saw a sudden, quick catch of breath in her throat; even as he looked the flush faded from her face, and she rose from her seat, her gaze still upon him.

"I - I am not feeling well," she said. "Will you please excuse me?"

In an instant Nome was at her side, but she turned quickly from him to the colonel, who had risen from his chair.

"Please take me to my room," she begged. "Then - then you can come back."

Once more her face turned to Steele. There was a pallor in it now that startled him. For a few moments he stood alone, as Breed and Nome left the table. He listened, and heard the opening and closing of a second door.

Then a footstep, and Nome reappeared.

"By Heaven, but she's a beauty!" he exclaimed. "I tell you, Steele -"

Something in his companion's eyes stopped him. Two red spots burned in Steele's cheeks as he advanced and gripped the other fiercely by the arm.

"Yes, she is pretty - very pretty," he said quietly, his fingers sinking deeper into Nome's arm. "Get your hat and coat, Nome. I want to see you in the cabin."

Behind them the door opened and closed again, and Steele shoved past his associate to meet Breed.

"Buck and I have a little matter to attend to over at the cabin," he explained. "When they - when the colonel returns tell him we'll be over to smoke an after-supper pipe with him a little later, will you? And give our compliments to - her." With a half-sneer on his lips he rejoined Nome, who stared hard at

James Oliver Curwood

him, and followed him through the outer door.

"Now, what the devil does this mean?" Nome demanded when they were outside. "If you have anything on your mind, Steele -"

"I have," interrupted Philip, "and I'm going to relieve myself of it. Pretty? She's as beautiful as an angel, Buck - the colonel's wife, I mean. And you - " He laughed harshly. "You're always the lucky dog, Buck Nome. You think she's half in love with you now. Too bad she was taken ill just at the psychological moment, as you might say, Buck. Wonder what was the matter?"

"Don't know," growled Nome, conscious of something in the other's voice which darkness concealed in his face.

"Of course, you don't," replied Steele.

"That's why I am bringing you over to the cabin. I am going to tell you just what happened when Mrs. Becker was taken ill, and when she turned a trifle pale, if you noticed sharply. Buck. It's a good joke, a mighty good joke, and I know you will thoroughly appreciate it."

He drew a step back when they came near the cabin, and Nome entered first. Very coolly Philip turned and bolted the door. Then, throwing off his coat, he pointed to the white skull dangling under the lamp.

"Allow me to introduce an old friend of mine, Buck - M'sieur Janette, of Nelson House."

With a sudden curse Nome leaped toward his companion, his face flaming, his hands clenched to strike - only to look into the shining muzzle of Steele's revolver, with Steele's cold gray eyes glittering dangerously behind it.

"Sit down, Nome - right there, under the man you killed!" he commanded. "Sit down, or by the gods I'll blow your head off where you stand! There - and I'll sit here, like this, so that the cur's heart within you is a bull's-eye for this gun. It's M'sieur Janette's turn tonight," he went on, leaning over the little table, the red spots in his cheeks growing redder and brighter as Nome cringed before his revolver. "M'sieur Janette's - and the colonel's; but mostly Janette's. Remember that, Nome. It's for Janette. I'm not thinking much about Mrs. Becker - just now."

Steele's breath came quickly and his lips were almost snarling in his hatred of the man before him.

"It's a lie!" gasped Nome chokingly, his face ashen white. "You lie when you say I killed - Janette."

The fingers of Steele's pistol hand twitched.

"How I'd like to kill you!" he breathed. "You won his wife, Nome; you broke his heart - and after that he killed himself. You sent a report into headquarters that he killed himself by accident. You lied. It was you who killed him - by taking his wife. I got his skull because I thought I might need it against you to show that it was a pistol instead of a rifle that killed him. And this isn't the first man you've sent to hell, Nome, and is isn't the first woman. But your next won't be Mrs. Becker!"

He thrust his revolver almost into the other man's face as Nome opened his lips to speak.

"Shut up!" he cried. "If you open your dirty mouth again I'll be tempted to kill you where you sit! Don't you know what happened to-night? Don't you know that Mrs. Becker forgot herself, and remembered again, just in time, and that you've taken a little blood from the colonel's heart as you took all of it from - his?" He reached up and broke the string that held the skull, turning the empty face of the thing toward Nome. "Look at it, you scoundrel! That's the man you killed, as you would kill the colonel if you could. That's Janette!"

His voice fell to a hissing whisper as he shoved the skull slowly across the table, so close that a sudden movement would have sent it against the other's breast.

"We've been fixing this thing up between us, Bucky - M'sieur Janette and I," he went on, "and we've come to the conclusion that we won't kill you, but that you don't belong to the service. Understand?"

"You mean - to drive me out - " One of Nome's hands had stolen to his side, and Steele's pistol arm grew tense.

"On the table with your hands, Bucky! There, that's better," he laughed softly.

"Yes, we're going to drive you out. You're going to pack up a few things right away, Bucky, and you're going to run like the devil away from this place. I'd advise you to go straight back to headquarters and resign from the Northwest Mounted. MacGregor knows you pretty well, Bucky, and knows one or two things you've done, even though your whole record is not an open book to him. I don't believe he'll put any obstacles in the way of your discharge although your enlistment hasn't expired. Disability is an easy plea, you know. But if the inspector should think so much of you that he is loath to let you go, then M'sieur Janette and I will have to fix up the story for headquarters, and I don't mind telling you we'll add just a little for interest, and that the woman and the people at Nelson House will swear to it. You've the making of a good outlaw, Bucky," he smiled tauntingly, "and if you follow your natural bent you'll have some of your old friends after you, good and hard. You'd better steer clear of that though, and try your hand at being honest for once. M'sieur Janette wants to give you this chance, and you'd better make good time. So get a move on, Bucky. You'll need a blanket and a little grub, that's all."

"Steele, you don't mean this! Good God, man -" Nome had half risen to his feet. "You don't mean this!"

With his free hand Philip took out his watch.

"I mean that if you are not gone within fifteen minutes I'll march you over to Breed and the colonel, tell them the story of M'sieur Janette, here, and hold you until we hear from headquarters," he said quickly. "Which will it be, Nome?"

Like one stunned by a blow Nome rose slowly to his feet. He spoke no word as he carefully filled his pack with the necessities of a long journey. At the door, as he opened it to go, he turned for just an instant upon Steele, who was still holding the revolver in his hand.

"Remember, Bucky," admonished Philip in a quiet voice, "it's all for the good of yourself and the service."

Fear had gone from Nome's face. It was filled now with a hatred so intense that his teeth shone like the fangs of a snarling animal.

"To hell with you," he said, "and to hell with the service; but remember, Philip Steele, remember that some day we'll meet again."

"Some day," laughed Philip. "Good-by, Bucky Nome - deserter!"

The door closed and Nome was gone.

"Now, M'sieur Janette, it's our turn," cried Steele, smiling companionably upon the skull and loading his pipe. "It's our turn."

He laughed aloud, and for some time puffed out luxurious clouds of smoke in silence.

"It's the best day's work I've done in my life," he continued, with his eyes still upon the skull. "The very best, and it would be complete, M'sieur, if I could send you down to the woman who helped to kill you."

He stopped, and his eyes leaped with a sudden fire. "By George!" he exclaimed, under his breath. His pipe went out; for many minutes he stared with set face at the skull, as if it had spoken to him and its voice had transfixed him where he stood. Then he tossed his pipe upon the table, collected his service equipment and strapped it in his pack. After that he returned to the table with a pad of paper and a pencil and sat down. His face was strangely white as he took the skull in his hands.

"I'll do it, so help me all the gods, I'll do it!" he breathed excitedly. "M'sieur, a woman killed you - as much as Bucky Nome, a woman did it. You couldn't do her any good - but you might - another. I'm going to send you to her, M'sieur. You're a terrible lesson, and I may be a beast; but you're preaching a powerful sermon, and I guess - perhaps - you may do her good. I'll tell her your story, old man, and the story of the woman who made you so nice and white and clean. Perhaps she'll see the moral, M'sieur. Eh? Perhaps!"

For a long time he wrote, and when he had done he sealed the writing, put the envelope and the skull together in a box, and tied the whole with babiche string. On the outside he fastened another note to Breed, the factor, in which he explained that he and Bucky Nome had found it necessary to leave that very night for the West. And he heavily underscored the lines in which he directed the factor to see that the box was delivered to Mrs. Colonel Becker, and that, as he valued the honor and the friendship of the service, and especially of Philip Steele, all knowledge of it should be kept from the colonel himself.

It was eight o'clock when he went out into the night with his pack upon his back. He grunted approval when he found it was snowing, for the track of himself and Nome would be covered. Through the thickening gloom the two or three lights in the factor's home gleamed like distant stars. One of them was brighter than the others, and he knew that it came from the rooms which Breed had fitted up for the colonel and his wife. As Philip halted for a moment, his eyes drawn by a haunting fascination to that window, the light grew clearer and brighter, and he fancied that he saw a face looking out into the night - toward his cabin. A moment later he knew that it was the woman's face. Then a door opened, and a figure hurried across the open. He stepped back into the gloom of his own cabin and waited. It was the colonel. Three times he knocked loudly at the cabin door.

"I'd like to go out and shake his hand," muttered Steele. "I'd like to tell him that he isn't the only man who's had an idol broken, and that Mrs. B.'s little flirtation isn't a circumstance - to what might have happened."

Instead, he moved silently away, and turned his face into the thin trail that buried itself in the black forests of the West.

CHAPTER IV

THE SILKEN SCARF

A loneliness deeper than he had ever known - a yearning that was almost pain, oppressed Philip as he left Lac Bain behind him. Half a mile from the post he stopped under a shelter of dense spruce, and stood listening as there came to him faintly the distant howling of a dog. After all, had he done right? He laughed harshly and his hands clenched as he thought of Bucky Nome. He had done right by him. But the skull - Mrs. Becker - was that right? Like a flash there came to him out of the darkness a picture of the scene beside the fire - of Mrs. Becker and the colonel, of the woman's golden head resting on her husband's shoulder, her sweet blue eyes filled with all the truth and glory of womanhood as she had looked up into his grizzled face. And then there took its place the scene beside the fire in the factor's room. He saw the woman's flushed cheeks as she listened to the low voice of Bucky Nome, he saw again what looked like yielding softness in her eyes - the grayish pallor in the colonel's face as he had looked upon the flirtation. Yes, he had done right. She had recovered herself in time, but she had taken a little bit of life from the colonel, and from him. She had broken his ideal - the ideal he had always hoped for, and had sought for, but had never found, and he told himself that now she was no better than the girl of the hyacinth letter, whose golden beauty and eyes as clear as an angel's had concealed this same deceit that wrecked men's lives. M'sieur Janette's clean, white skull and the story of how and why M'sieur Janette had died would not be too great a punishment for her.

He resumed his journey, striving to concentrate his mind on other things. Seven or eight miles to the south and west was the cabin of Jacques Pierrot, a half-breed, who had a sledge and dogs. He would hire Jacques to accompany him on his patrol in place of Bucky Nome. Then he would return to Nelson House and send in his report of Bucky Nome's desertion, since he knew well enough after the final remarks of that gentleman that he did not intend to sever his connection with the Northwest Mounted in the regular way. After that - He shrugged his shoulders as he thought of the fourteen months' of service still ahead of him. Until now his adventure as a member of the Royal Mounted had not grown monotonous for an hour. Excitement, action, fighting against odds, had been the spice of life to him, and he struggled to throw off the change that had taken hold of him the moment he had opened the hyacinth-scented letter of Mrs. Becker. "You're a fool," he argued. "You're as big a fool as Bucky Nome. My God - you - Phil Steele - letting a married woman upset you like this!"

It was near midnight when he came to Pierrot's cabin, but a light was still burning in the half-breed's log home. Philip kicked off his snow shoes and knocked at the door. In a moment Pierrot opened it, stepped back, and stared at the white figure that came in out of the storm.

"Mon Dieu - it ees you - Mee-sair Philip!"

Philip held out his hand to Jacques, and shot a quick glance about him. There had been a change in the cabin since he had visited it last. One of Pierrot's hands was done up in a sling, his face was thin and pale, and his dark eyes were sunken and lusterless. In the little wilderness home there was an air of desertion and neglect, and Philip wondered where Pierrot's rosy-cheeked, black-haired wife and his half dozen children had gone.

James Oliver Curwood

"Mon Dieu - it ees you, Mee-sair Philip," cried Pierrot again, his face lighting up with pleasure. "You come late. You are hongree?"

"I've had supper," replied Philip. "I've just come from Lac Bain. But what's up, old man -?" He pointed to Pierrot's hand, and looked questionably about the cabin again.

"Eh - Iowla - my wife - she is at Churchill, over on the bay," groaned Jacques. "And so are the children. What! You did not hear at Lac Bain? Iowla is taken seek - ver' seek - with a strange thing which - ugh! - has to be fixed with a knife, Mee-sair Philip. An' so I take her to the doctor over at Churchill, an' he fix her - an' she is growing well now, an' will soon come home. She keep the children with her. She say they mak' her think of Jacques, on his trap-line. Eh - it ees lonely - dam' - dam' lonely, and I have been gone from my Iowla but two weeks to-morrow."

"You have been with her at Fort Churchill?" asked Philip, taking off his pack and coat.

"Oui, M'sieur," said Jacques, falling into his French. "I have been there since November. What! They did not tell you at Lac Bain?"

"No - they did not tell me. But I was there but a few hours, Jacques. Listen -" He pulled out his pipe and began filling it, with his back to the stove. "You saw people - strangers - at Fort Churchill, Jacques? They came over on the London ship, and among them there was a woman -"

Pierrot's pale face flashed up with sudden animation.

"Ah - zee angel!" he cried. "That is what my Iowla called her, M'sieur. See!" He pointed to his bandaged hand. "Wan day that bete - the Indian dog of mine - did that, an' w'en I jumped up from the snow in front of the company's store, the blood running from me, I see her standing there, white an' scared. An' then she run to me with a little scream, an' tear something from her neck, an' tie it round my hand. Then she go with me to my cabin, and every day after that she come to see my Iowla an' the children. She wash little Pierre, an' cut his hair. She wash Jean an' Mabelle. She laugh an' sing an' hol' the baby, an' my Iowla laugh an' sing; an' she takes down my Iowla's hair, which is so long that it falls to her knees, an' does it up in a wonderful way an' says she would give everything she got if she could have that hair. An' my Iowla laugh at her, because her hair is like an angel's - like fire w'en the sun is on it; an' my Iowla tak' hers down, all red an' gold, an' do it up in the Cree way. And w'en she brings the man with her - he laughs an' plays with the kids, an' says he knows the doctor and that there will be nothing to pay for all that he is done. Ah - she ees wan be-e-eautiful-l-l angel! An' this - this is w'at she tied around my hand."

With new life Pierrot went to a covered box nailed against one of the log walls and a moment later placed in Philip's hands a long, white, silken neck-scarf. Once more there rose to his nostrils the sweet, faint scent of hyacinth, and with a sudden low cry Philip crushed the dainty fabric in a mass to his face. In that moment it seemed as though the sweetness of the woman herself was with him, stirring him at last to confess the truth - the thing which he had fought against so fiercely in those few hours at Lac Bain; and the knowledge that he had surrendered to himself, that in going from Lac Bain he was leaving all that the world held for him in the way of woman and love, drew his breath from him in another broken, stifled cry.

When he lowered the scarf his face was white. Pierrot was staring at him.

"It makes me think - of home," he explained lamely. "Sometimes I get lonely, too. There's a girl - down there - who wears a scarf like this, and what she wears smells like a flower, just as this does -"

"Oui, I understand," said Pierrot softly. "It is the way I feel when my Iowla is gone."

He replaced the scarf in the box, and when he returned to the stove Philip explained why he had come to his cabin. With Pierrot's promise to accompany him with dogs and sledge on his patrol the next day he prepared to go to bed. Pierrot also was undressing, and Philip said to him casually,

"This woman - at Churchill - Jacques - what if some one should tell you that she is not so much of an angel after all - that she is, perhaps, something like - like the woman over at Lac la Biche, who ran away with the Englishman?"

Pierrot straightened as though Philip had thrust a knife-point into his back. He broke forth suddenly into French.

"I would call him a liar, M'sieur," he cried fiercely. "I would call him a liar, once-twice - three times, and then if he said it again I would fight him. Mon Dieu, but it would be no sin to kill one with a mouth like that!"

Philip was conscious of the hot blood rushing to his face as he bent over his bunk. The depths of Pierrot's faith shamed him, and he crawled silently between the blankets and turned his face to the wall. Pierrot extinguished the light, and a little later Philip could hear his deep breathing. But sleep refused to close his own eyes, and he lay on his back, painfully awake. In spite of the resolution he had made to think no more of the woman at Lac Bain, his mind swept him back to her irresistibly. He recalled every incident that had occurred, every word that she had spoken, since he had first looked upon her beautiful face out on the Churchill trail. He could find nothing but purity and sweetness until he came with her for that fatal hour or two into the company of Bucky Nome. And then, again, his blood grew hot. But - after all - was there not some little excuse for her? He thought of the hundreds of women he had known, and wondered if there was one among them all who had not at some time fallen into this same little error as Mrs. Becker. For the first time he began to look at himself. Mrs. Becker had laughed with Bucky Nome, her cheeks had grown a little flushed, her eyes had shone radiantly - but were those things a sin? Had those same eyes not looked up into his own, filled with a sweetness that thrilled him, when he bent over her beside the fire out on the Churchill trail? Was there not that same lovely flush in her face when his lips had almost touched her hair? And had not the colonel's sudden return brought a flush into both their faces? He smiled to himself, and for a moment he thrilled ecstatically. The reaction came like a shock. In an instant other scenes - other faces - flashed upon him, and again he saw the luring, beautiful face of Eileen Hawkins, who smiled on men as Mrs. Becker had smiled on Bucky Nome and on him.

He closed his eyes and tried to force himself into sleep, but failed. At last he rose silently from his bunk, filled his pipe, and sat down in the darkness beside the stove. The storm had increased to a gale, wailing and moaning over the cabin outside, and the sound carried him back to the last night in the cabin far to the south, when he had destroyed the hyacinth-scented letter. The thought of the letter moved him restlessly. He listened to Pierrot's breathing, and knew that the half-breed was asleep. Then he rose to his feet and laid his pipe on the table. A curious feeling of guilt came over him as he moved toward the box in which Jacques had placed the silken scarf. His breath came quickly; in the dark his eyes shone; a tingling thrill of strange pleasure shot through him as his fingers touched the thing for which they were searching. He drew the scarf out, and returned to the stove with it, crushing it in both his hands. The sweetness of it came to him again like the woman's breath. It was the sweetness of her hair, of the golden coils massed in the firelight; a part of the woman herself, of her glorious eyes, her lips, her face - and suddenly he crushed the fabric to his own face, and stood there, trembling in the darkness, while Jacques Pierrot slept and the storm wailed and moaned over his head. For he knew - now - that he would do more for this woman than Jacques Pierrot could ever do; more, perhaps, than even the colonel, her husband, would do. His

James Oliver Curwood

heart seemed bursting with a new and terrible pain, and the truth at last seemed to rise and choke him. He loved her. He loved this woman, the wife of another man. He loved her as he had never dreamed that he could love a woman, and with the scarf still smothering his lips and face he stood for many minutes, silent and motionless, gathering himself slowly from out of the appalling depths into which he had allowed himself to plunge.

Then he folded the scarf, and instead of returning it to the box, put it in one of the pockets of his coat.

"Pierrot won't care," he excused himself. "And it's the only thing, little girl - the only thing - I'll ever have - of you."

CHAPTER V

BEAUTY-PROOF

It was Pierrot who aroused Philip in the morning.

"Mon, Dieu, but you have slept like a bear," he exclaimed. "The storm has cleared and it will be fine traveling. Eh - you have not heard? I wonder why they are firing guns off toward Lac Bain!"

Philip jumped from his bed, and his first look was in the direction of the box. He was criminal enough to hope that Jacques would not discover that the scarf was missing.

"A moose - probably," he said. "There were tracks close up to the post a day or two ago."

He was anxious to begin their journey, and assisted Pierrot in preparing breakfast. The sound of guns impressed upon him the possibility of some one from Lac Bain calling at the half-breed's cabin, and he wished to avoid further association with people from the post - at least for a time. At nine o'clock Pierrot bolted the door and the two set off into the south and west. On the third day they swung to the eastward to strike the Indians living along Reindeer Lake, and on the sixth cut a trail by compass straight for Nelson House. A week later they arrived at the post, and Philip found a letter awaiting him calling him to Prince Albert. In a way the summons was a relief to him. He bade Pierrot good-by, and set out for Le Pas in company with two Indians. From that point he took the work train to Etomami, and three hours later was in Prince Albert.

"Rest up for a time, Steele," Inspector MacGregor told him, after he had made a personal report on Bucky Nome.

During the week that followed Philip had plenty of leisure in which to tell himself that he was a fool, and that he was deliberately throwing away what a munificent fortune had placed in his hands. MacGregor's announcement that he was in line for promotion in the near future did not stir him as it would have done a few weeks before. In his little barracks room he laughed ironically as he recalled MacGregor's words, "We're going to make a corporal or a sergeant of you." He - Philip Steele - millionaire, club man, son of a western king of finance - a corporal or a sergeant! For the first time the thought amused him, and then it maddened him. He had played the part of an idiot, and all because there had been born within him a love of adventure and the big, free life of the open. No wonder some of his old club friends regarded him as a scapegrace and a ne'er-do-well. He had thrown away position, power, friends and home as carelessly as he might have tossed away the end of a cigar. And all - for this! He looked about his cramped quarters, a half sneer on his lips. He had tied himself to this! To his ears there came faintly the thunder of galloping hoofs. Sergeant Moody was training his rookies to ride. The sneer left his lips, and was replaced by a quick, alert smile as he heard a rattle of revolver shots and the cheering of voices. After all, it was not so bad. It was a service that made men, and he thought of the English remittance-man, whose father was a lord of something-or-other, and who was learning to ride and shoot out there with red-headed, raucous-voiced Moody. There began to stir in him again the old desire for action, and he was glad when word was sent to him that Inspector MacGregor wished to see him in his office.

The big inspector was pacing back and forth when Philip came in.

"Sit down, Steele, sit down," he said. "Take it easy, man - and have a cigar."

If MacGregor had suddenly gone into a fit Philip could not have been more surprised than at these words, as he stood with his cap in his hand before the desk of the fiery-mustached inspector, who was passing his box of choice Havanas. There are tightly drawn lines of distinction in the Royal Mounted. As Philip had once heard the commissioner say, "Every man in the service is a king - but there are different degrees of kings," and for a barracks man to be asked to sit in the inspector's office and smoke was a sensational breach of the usual code. But as he had distinctly heard the invitation to sit, and to smoke, Philip proceeded to do both, and waited in silence for the next mine to explode under his feet. And there was a certain ease in his manner of doing these things which would have assured most men that he was not unaccustomed to sitting in the presence of greatness.

The inspector seemed to notice this. For a moment he stood squarely in front of Steele, his hands shoved deep into his pockets, a twinkle in the cold, almost colorless eyechuckling, companionable laugh, such as finds its vent in the fellowship of equals, but which is seldom indulged in by a superior before an inferior in the R.N.W.M. Police.

"Mighty good cigars, eh, Steele?" he asked, turning slowly toward the window. "The commissioner sent 'em up to me from Regina. Nothing like a good cigar on a dreary day like this. Whew, listen to the wind - straight from Medicine Hat!"

For a few moments he looked out upon the cheerless drab roofs of the barracks, with their wisps of pale smoke swirling upward into the leaden sky; counted the dozen gnarled and scrubby trees, as had become a habit with him; rested his eyes upon the black and shriveled remnants of summer flower-beds thrusting their frost-shrunken stalks through the snow, and then, almost as if he were speaking to himself, he said, "Steele, are you beautyproof?"

There was no banter in his voice. It was low, so low that it had in it the ring of something more than mere desire for answer, and when the inspector turned, Philip observed a thing that he had never seen before - a flush in MacGregor's face. His pale eyes gleamed. His voice was filled with an intense earnestness as he repeated the question. "I want to know, Steele. Are you beauty-proof?"

In spite of himself Philip felt the fire rising in his own face. In that moment the inspector could have hit on no words that would have thrilled him more deeply than those which he had spoken. Beauty-proof! Did MacGregor know? Was it possible - He took a step forward, words came to his lips, but he caught himself before he had given voice to them.

Beauty-proof!

He laughed, softly, as the inspector had laughed a few moments before. But there was a strange tenseness in his face - something which MacGregor saw, but could not understand.

"Beauty-proof?" He repeated the words, looking keenly at the other. "Yes, I think I am, sir."

"You think you are?"

"I am quite sure that I am. Inspector. That is as far as I can go."

The inspector seated himself at his desk and opened a drawer. From it he took a photograph. For some time he gazed at it in silence, puffing out clouds of smoke from his cigar. Then, without lifting his eyes from the picture, he said: "I am going to put you up against a queer case, Steele, and the strangest thing about it is its very simplicity. It's a job for the greenest rookie in the service, and yet I swear that there isn't another man in Saskatchewan to whom I would talk as I am about to talk to you. Rather paradoxical, isn't it?"

"Rather," agreed Philip.

"And yet not when you come to understand the circumstances," continued the inspector, placing the photograph face down on the table and looking at the other through a purple cloud of tobacco smoke. "You see, Steele, I know who you are. I know that your father is Philip Steele, the big Chicago banker. I know that you are up here for romance and adventure rather than for any other thing there is in the service. I know, too, that you are no prairie chicken, and that most of your life has been spent where you see beautiful women every hour of the day, and where soft voices and tender smiles aren't the most wonderful things in the world, as they sometimes are up here. Fact is, we have a way of our own of running down records -"

"And a confounded clever one it must be," interrupted Philip irreverently. "Had you any - any particular reason for supposing me to be 'beauty-proof,' as you call it?" he added coldly.

"I've told you my only reason," said the inspector, leaning over his desk. "You've seen so many pretty faces, Steele, and you've associated with them so long that one up here isn't going to turn your head. Now -"

MacGregor hesitated, and laughed. The flush grew deeper in his cheeks, and he looked again at the photograph.

"I'm going to be frank with you," he went on. "This young woman called on me yesterday, and within a quarter of an hour - fifteen minutes, mind you! - she had me going like a fool! Understand? I'm not proof - against her - and yet I'm growing old in the service and haven't had a love affair since - a long time ago. I'm going to send you up to the Wekusko camp, above Le Pas, to bring down a prisoner. The man is her husband, and he almost killed Hodges, who is chief of construction up there. The minimum he'll get is ten years, and this woman is moving heaven and earth to save him. So help me God, Steele, if I was one of the youngsters, and she came to me as she did yesterday, I believe I'd let him give me the slip! But it mustn't happen. Understand? It mustn't happen. We've got to bring that man down, and we've got to give him the law. Simple thing, isn't it - this bringing a prisoner down from Wekusko! Any rookie could do it, couldn't he? And yet -"

The inspector paused to light his cigar, which had gone out. Then he added: "If you'll do this, Steele - and care for it - I'll see that you get your promotion."

As he finished, he tossed the photograph across the desk. "That's she. Don't ask me how I got the picture."

A curious thrill shot through Philip as he picked up the bit of cardboard. It was a wondrously sweet face that looked squarely out of it into his eyes, a face so youthful, so filled with childish prettiness that an exclamation of surprise rose to his lips. Under other circumstances he would have sworn that it was the picture of a school-girl. He looked up, about to speak, but MacGregor had turned again to the window, clouds of smoke about his head. He spoke without turning his head.

"That was taken nearly ten years ago," he said, and Philip knew that he was making an effort to keep an unnatural break out of his voice. "But there has been little change - almost none. His name is Thorpe. I will send you a written order this afternoon and you can start to-night."

Philip rose, and waited.

"Is there nothing more?" he asked, after a moment. "This woman -"

"There is nothing more," interrupted the inspector, still looking out through the window.

"Only this, Steele - you must bring him back. Whatever happens, bring back your prisoner."

As he turned to leave, Philip fancied that he caught something else - a stifled, choking breath, a sound that made him turn his head again as he went through the door. The inspector had not moved.

"Now what the deuce does this mean?" he asked himself, closing the door softly behind him. "You're up against something queer this time, Philip Steele, I'll wager dollars to doughnuts. Promotion for bringing in a prisoner! What in thunder -"

He stopped for a moment in one of the cleared paths. From the big low roofed drill enclosure a hundred yards away came the dull thud of galloping hoofs and the voice of Sergeant Moody thundering instructions to the rookies. Moody had a heart like flint and would have faced blazing cannon to perform his duty. He had grown old and ugly in the service and was as beauty-proof as an ogre of stone. Why hadn't MacGregor sent him?

Beauty-proof! The words sent a swift rush of thought, of regret, of the old homesickness and longing through Philip as he returned to his quarters. He wondered just how much MacGregor knew, and he sat down to bring up before him for the thousandth time a vision of the two faces that had played their part in his life - the face of the girl at home, as beautiful as a Diane de Poitiers, as soulless as a sphinx, who had offered herself to him in return for his name and millions, and of that other which he had met away up in the frozen barrens of Lac Bain. Beauty-proof! He laughed and loaded his pipe. MacGregor had made a good guess, even though he did not know what had passed that winter before he came north to seek adventure, or of the fight he had made for another woman, with Mr. Bucky Nome - deserter!

CHAPTER VI

PHILIP FOLLOWS A PRETTY FACE

It was late in the afternoon when Philip's instructions came from the inspector. They were tersely official in form, gave him all necessary authority, and ordered him to leave for Le Pas that night. Pinned to the order was a small slip of paper, and on this MacGregor had repeated in writing his words of a few hours before: "Whatever happens, bring back your prisoner."

There was no signature to this slip, and the first two words were heavily underscored. What did this double caution mean? Coming from a man like MacGregor, who was as choice as a king of his advice, Philip knew that it was of unusual significance. If it was intended as a warning, why had not the inspector given him more detail? During the hour in which he was preparing for his journey he racked his brain for some clew to the situation. The task which he was about to perform seemed simple enough. A man named Thorpe had attempted murder at Wekusko. He was already a prisoner, and he was to bring him down. The biggest coward in Saskatchewan, or a man from a hospital bed, could do this much, and yet -

He read the inspector's words over and over again. "Whatever happens!" In spite of himself a little stir of excitement crept into his blood. Since that thrilling hour in which he had seen Bucky Nome desert from the service he had not felt himself moved as now, and in a moment of mental excitement he found himself asking a question which a few minutes before he would have regarded as a mark of insanity. Was it possible that in the whole of the Northland there could be another woman as beautiful as Colonel Becker's wife - a woman so beautiful that she had turned even Inspector MacGregor's head, as Mrs. Becker had turned Bucky Nome's - and his? Was it possible that between these two women - between this wife of an attempted murderer and Mrs. Becker there was some connecting link - some association -

He cut his thoughts short with a low exclamation of disgust. The absurdity of the questions he had asked himself brought a flush into his face. But he could not destroy the undercurrent of emotions they had aroused. Anyway, something was going to happen. He was sure of that. The inspector's actions, his words, his mysterious nervousness, the strange catch in his voice as they parted, all assured him that there was a good reason for the repeated warning. And whatever did happen was to be brought about by the woman whose girlish beauty he had looked upon in the picture. That MacGregor was aware of the nature of his peril, if he was to run into danger at all, he was sure, and he was equally certain that some strong motive restrained the inspector from saying more than he had. Already he began to scent in the adventure ahead of him those elements of mystery, of excitement, even of romance, the craving for which was an inherited part of his being. And with these things there came another sensation, one that surprised and disquieted him. A few days before his one desire had been to get out of the north country, to place as much distance as possible between himself and Lac Bain. And now he found himself visibly affected by the thought that his duty was to take him once more in the direction of the woman whose sweet face had become an indissoluble part of his existence. He would not see her. Even at Wekusko he would be many days' journey from Lac Bain. But she would be nearer to him, and it was this that quickened his pulse.

He was ten minutes early for his train, and employed that interval in mingling among the people at the station.

MacGregor had as much as told him that whatever unusual thing might develop depended entirely upon the appearance of the woman and he began to look for her. She was not at the station. Twice he walked through the coaches of his train without discovering a face that resembled that in the photograph.

It was late when he arrived at Etomami, where the sixty mile line of the Hudson's Bay Railroad branches off to the north. At dawn he entered the caboose of the work train, which was to take him up through the wilderness to Le Pas. He was the only passenger.

"There ain't even a hand-car gone up ahead of us," informed the brakeman in response to his inquiry. "This is the only train in five days."

After all, it was to be a tame affair, in spite of the inspector's uneasiness and warnings, thought Philip. The woman was not ahead of him. Two days before she had been in MacGregor's office, and under the circumstances it was impossible for her to be at Le Pas or at Wekusko, unless she had traveled steadily on dog sledge. Philip swore softly to himself in his disappointment, ate breakfast with the train gang, went to sleep, and awoke when they plowed their way into the snow-smothered outpost on the Saskatchewan.

The brakeman handed him a letter.

"This came on the Le Pas mail," he explained. "I kept it out for you instead of sending it to the office."

"Thank you," said Philip. "A special - from headquarters. Why in thunder didn't they send me a messenger instead of a letter, Braky? They could have caught me on the train."

He tore open the departmental envelope as he spoke and drew forth a bit of folded paper. It was not the official letter-head, but at a glance Philip recognized the inspector's scrawling writing and his signature. It was one of MacGregor's quiet boasts that the man did not live who could forge his name. An astonished whistle broke from his lips as he read these few lines:

Follow your conscience, whatever you do. Both God and man will reward you in the end.

Felix MacGregor.

And this was all. There was no date, no word of explanation; even his own name had been omitted from this second order. He picked up the envelope which had fallen to the floor and looked at the postmark. It had been stamped four-thirty. It was after five, an hour later, that he had received his verbal instructions from MacGregor! The inspector must have written the note before their interview of the preceding afternoon - before his repeated injunction of "Whatever happens, bring back your prisoner!" But this letter was evidently intended as final instructions since it had been sent so as to reach him at this time. What did it mean? The question buzzed in Philip's brain, repeated itself twenty times, fifty times, as he hurried through the gathering darkness of the semi-polar night toward the log hotel of the place. He was convinced that there was some hidden motive in the inspector's actions. What was he to understand?

Suddenly he stopped, a hundred yards from the glimmering lights of the Little Saskatchewan hotel, and chuckled audibly as he stuffed his pipe. It flashed upon him now why MacGregor had chosen him instead of an ordinary service man to bring down the prisoner from Wekusko. MacGregor knew that he, Philip Steele, college man and man of the world, would reason out the key to this little puzzle, whereas Sergeant Moody and others of his type would turn back for explanations. And Inspector MacGregor, twenty years in the service, and recognized as the shrewdest man-hunter between the coasts, wished to give no explanation. Philip's blood tingled with fresh excitement as the tremendous risk which the inspector himself was running, dawned upon him. Publicity of the note which he held in his hand would mean the disgrace and retirement even of Felix MacGregor.

He thrust the letter in his pocket and hurried on. The lights of the settlement were already agleam. From the edge of the frozen river there came the sound of a wheezy accordion in a Chinese cafe, and the howling of a dog, either struck by man or worsted in a fight. Where the more numerous lights of the one street shone red against the black background of forest, a drunken half-breed was chanting in half-Cree, half-French, the chorus of the caribou song. He heard the distant snapping of a whip, the yelping response of huskies, and a moment later a sledge and six dogs passed him so close that he was compelled to leap from their path. This was Le Pas - the wilderness! Beyond it, just over the frozen river which lay white and silent before him, stretched that endless desolation of romance and mystery which he had grown to love, a world of deep snows, of silent-tongued men, of hardship and battle for life where the law of nature was the survival of the fittest, and that of man, "Do unto others as ye would that they should do unto you." Never did Philip Steele's heart throb with the wild, free pulse of life and joy as in such moments as these, when his fortune, his clubs, and his friends were a thousand miles away, and he stood on the edge of the big northern Unknown.

As he had slept through the trainmen's dinner hour, he was as hungry as a wolf, and he lost no time in seating himself in a warm corner of the low, log-ceilinged dining-room of the Little Saskatchewan. Although a quarter of an hour early, he had hardly placed himself at his table when another person entered the room. Casually he glanced up from the two letters which he had spread out before him. The one who had followed him was a woman. She had turned sharply upon seeing him and seated herself at the next table, her back so toward him that he caught only her half profile.

It was enough to assure him that she was young and pretty. On her head she wore a turban of silver lynx fur, and about this she had drawn her glossy brown hair, which shone like burnished copper in the lamp-glow, and had gathered it in a bewitchingly coquettish knot low on her neck, where it shone with a new richness and a new warmth with every turn of her head. But not once did she turn so that Philip could see more than the tantalizing pink of her cheek and the prettiness of her chin, which at times was partly concealed in a collarette of the same silver gray lynx fur.

He ate his supper almost mechanically, in spite of his hunger, for his mind was deep in the mysterious problem which confronted him. Half a dozen times he broke in upon his thoughts to glance at the girl at the opposite table. Once he was sure that she had been looking at him and that she had turned just in time to keep her face from him. Philip admired pretty women, and of all beauty in woman he loved beautiful hair, so that more and more frequently his eyes traveled to the shining wealth of copper-colored tresses near him. He had almost finished his supper when a movement at the other table drew his eyes up squarely, and his heart gave a sudden jump. The girl had risen. She was facing him, and as for an instant their eyes met she hesitated, as if she were on the point of speaking. In that moment he recognized her.

It was the girl in the photograph, older, more beautiful - the same soft, sweet contour of face, the same dark eyes that had looked at him in MacGregor's office, filled with an indescribable sadness now, instead of the laughing joy of girlhood. In another moment he would have responded to her hesitation, to the pathetic tremble of her lips, but before words could form themselves she had turned and was gone. And yet at the door, even as she disappeared, he saw her face turned to him again, pleadingly, entreatingly, as if she knew his mission and sent to him a silent prayer for mercy.

Thrusting back his chair, he caught up his hat from a rack and followed. He was in time to see her pass through the low door out into the night. Without hesitation his mind had leaped to a definite purpose. He would overtake her outside, introduce himself, and then perhaps he would understand the conflicting orders of Inspector MacGregor.

The girl was passing swiftly down the main street when he took up the pursuit. Suddenly she turned into a path dug through the snow that led riverward. Ahead of her there was only the starlit gloom of night and the distant blackness of the wilderness edge. Philip's blood ran a little faster. She had expected that he would follow, knew that he was close behind her, and had turned down into this deserted place that they might not be observed! He made no effort now to overtake her, but kept the same distance between them, whistling carelessly and knowing that she would stop to wait for him. Ahead of them there loomed up out of the darkness a clump of sapling spruce, and into their shadow the girl disappeared.

A dozen paces more and Philip himself was buried in the thick gloom. He heard quick, light footsteps in the snow-crust ahead of him. Then there came another sound - a step close behind him, a noise of disturbed brush, a low voice which was not that of a woman, and before his hand could slip, to the holster at his belt a human form launched itself upon him from the side, and a second form from behind, and under their weight he fell a helpless heap into the snow. Powerful hands wrenched his arms behind his back and other hands drew a cloth about his mouth. A stout cord was twisted around his wrists, his legs were tied, and then his captors relieved him of their weight.

Not a word had been spoken during the brief struggle. Not a word was spoken now as his mysterious assailants hoisted him between them and followed in the footsteps of the woman. Scarcely a hundred paces beyond the spruce the dark shadow of a cabin came into view. Into this he was carried and placed on something which he took to be a box. Then a light was struck.

For the first time Philip's astonished eyes had a view of his captors. One of them was an old man, a giant in physique, with a long gray beard and grayish yellow hair that fell to his shoulders. His companion was scarcely more than a boy, yet in his supple body, as he moved about, Philip recognized the animal-like strength of the forest breed. A word spoken in a whisper by the boy revealed the fact that the two were father and son. From that side of the room which was at Philip's back they dragged forth a long pine box, and were engaged in this occupation when the door opened and a third man entered. Never had Philip looked on a more unprepossessing face than that of the newcomer, in whose little black eyes there seemed to be a gloating triumph as he leered at the prisoner. He was short, with a huge breadth of shoulders. His eyes and mouth and nose were all but engulfed in superfluous flesh, and as he turned from Philip to the man and boy over the box he snapped the joints of his fingers in a startling manner.

"Howdy, howdy!" he wheezed, like one afflicted with asthma. "Good! good!" With these four words he lapsed into the silence of the older man and the boy.

As the box was dragged full into the light, a look of horror shot into Philip's eyes. It was the rough-box of a coffin! Without a word, and apparently without a signal, the three surrounded him and lifted him bodily into it. To his surprise he found himself lying upon something soft, as if the interior of his strange prison had been padded with cushions. Then, with extreme caution, his arms were freed from under his back and strapped to his side, and other straps, broad and firm, were fastened from side to side of the box across his limbs and body, as if there were danger of his flying up and out through the top. Another moment and a shadow fell above him, pitch gloom engulfed him.

They were dragging on the cover to the box! He heard the rapid beating of a hammer, the biting of nails into wood, and he writhed and struggled to free his hands, to cry out, to gain the use of his legs, but not the fraction of an inch could he relieve himself of his fetters. After a time his straining muscles relaxed, and he stopped to get his breath and listen. Faintly there came to him the sound of subdued voices, and he caught

James Oliver Curwood

a glimmer of light, then another, and still a third. He saw now that half a dozen holes had been bored into the cover and sides of the box. The discovery brought with it a sense of relief. At least he was not to be suffocated. He found, after an interval, that he was even comfortable, and that his captors had not only given him a bed to lie upon, but had placed a pillow under his head.

CHAPTER VII

THE TRAGEDY IN THE CABIN

A few moments later Philip heard the movement of heavy feet, the opening and closing of a door, and for a time after that there was silence. Had MacGregor anticipated this, he wondered? Was this a part of the program which the inspector had foreseen that he would play? His blood warmed at the thought and he clenched his fists. Then he began to think more calmly. His captors had not relieved him of his weapons. They had placed his service cap in the box with him and had unbuckled his cartridge belt so that he would rest more comfortably. What did all this mean? For the hundredth time he asked himself the question.

Returning footsteps interrupted his thoughts. The cabin door opened, people entered, again he heard whispering voices.

He strained his ears. At first he could have sworn that he heard the soft, low tones of a woman's voice, but they were not repeated. Hands caught hold of the box, dragged it across the floor, and then he felt himself lifted bodily, and, after a dozen steps, placed carefully upon some object in the snow. His amazement increased when he understood what was occurring.

He was on a sledge. Through the air-holes in his prison he heard the scraping of strap-thongs as they were laced through the runner-slits and over the box, the restless movement of dogs, a gaping whine, the angry snap of a pair of jaws. Then, slowly, the sledge began to move. A whip cracked loudly above him, a voice rose in a loud shout, and the dogs were urged to a trot. Again there came to Philip's ears the wheezing notes of the accordion. By a slight effort he found that he could turn his head sufficiently to look through a hole on a level with his eyes in the side of the box. The sledge had turned from the dark trail into the lighted street, and stopped at last before a brilliantly lighted front from which there issued the sound of coarse voices, of laughter and half-drunken song.

One of his captors went into the bar while the other seated himself on the box, with one leg shutting out Philip's vision by dangling it over the hole through which he was looking.

"What's up, Fingy?" inquired a voice.

"Wekusko," replied the man on the box, in the husky, flesh-smothered tones of the person who had entered last into the cabin.

"Another dead one up there, eh?" persisted the same voice.

"No. Maps 'n' things f'r Hodges, up at the camp. Devil of a hurry, ain't he, to order us up at night? Tell - to hustle out with the bottle, will you?"

The speaker sent the lash of his whip snapping through the air in place of supplying a name.

"Maps and things - for Hodges - Wekusko!" gasped Philip inwardly.

He listened for further information. None came, and soon the man called Fingy jumped from the box, cracked his whip with a wheezing command to the dogs, and the sledge moved on.

And so his captors were taking him to Wekusko? - and more than that, to Hodges, chief of construction, whose life had been attempted by the prisoner whom Inspector MacGregor had ordered him to bring down! Had Fingy spoken the truth? And, if so, was this another part of the mysterious plot foreseen by the inspector?

During the next half hour, in which the sledge traveled steadily over the smooth, hard trail into the north, Philip asked himself these and a score of other questions equally perplexing. He was certain that the beautiful young woman whom he had followed had purposely lured him into the ambush. He considered himself her prisoner. Then why should he be consigned, like a parcel of freight, to Hodges, her husband's accuser, and the man who demanded the full penalty of the law for his assailant?

The more he added to the questions that leaped into his mind the more mystified he became. The conflicting orders, the strange demeanor of his chief, the pathetic appeal that he had seen in the young woman's eyes, the ambush, and now this unaccountable ride to Wekusko, strapped in a coffin box, all combined to plunge him into a chaos of wonder from which it was impossible for him to struggle forth. However, he assured himself of two things; he was comparatively comfortable, and within two hours at the most they would reach Hodges' headquarters, if the Wekusko camp were really to be their destination. Something must develop then.

It had ceased to occur to him that there was peril in his strange position. If that were so, would his captors have left him in possession of his weapons, even imprisoned as he was? If they had intended him harm, would they have cushioned his box and placed a pillow under his head so that the cloth about his mouth would not cause him discomfort? It struck him as peculiarly significant, now that he had suffered no injury in the short struggle on the trail, that no threats or intimidation had been offered after his capture. This was a part of the game which he was to play! He became more and more certain of it as the minutes passed, and there occurred to him again and again the inspector's significant words, "Whatever happens!" MacGregor had spoken the words with particular emphasis, had repeated them more than once. Were they intended to give him a warning of this, to put him on his, guard, as well as at his ease?

And with these thoughts, many, conflicting and mystifying, he found it impossible to keep from associating other thoughts of Bucky Nome, and of the woman whom he now frankly confessed to himself that he loved. If conditions had been a little different, if the incidents had not occurred just as they had, he have suspected the hand of Bucky Nome in what was transpiring now. But he discarded that suspicion the instant that it came to him. That which remained with him more and more deeply as the minutes passed was a mental picture of the two women - of this woman who was fighting to save her husband, and of the other, whom he loved, and for whom he had fought to save her for her husband. It was with a dull feeling of pain that he compared the love, the faith, and the honor of this woman whose husband had committed a crime with that one night's indiscretion of Mrs. Becker. It was in her eyes and face that he had seen a purity like that of an angel, and the pain seemed to stab him deeper when he thought that, after all, it was the criminal's wife who was proving herself, not Mrs. Becker.

He strove to unburden his mind for a time, and turned his head so that he could peer through the hole in the side of the box. The moon had risen, and now and then he caught flashes of the white snow in the opens, but more frequently only the black shadows of the forest through which they were passing. They had not left Le Pas more than two hours behind when the sledge stopped again and Philip saw a few scattered lights a short distance away.

"Must be Wekusko," he thought. "Hello, what's that?"

A voice came sharply from the opposite side of the box.

"Is that you, Fingy?" it demanded. "What the devil have you got there?"

"Your maps and things, sir," replied Fingy hoarsely. "Couldn't come up to-morrow, so thought we'd do it to-night."

Philip heard the closing of a door, and footsteps crunched in the snow close to his ears.

"Love o' God!" came the voice again. "What's this you've brought them up in, Fingy?"

"Coffin box, sir. Only thing the maps'd fit into, and it's been layin' around useless since MacVee kem down in it Mebby you can find use for it, later," he chuckled grewsomely. "Ho-ho-ho! mebby you can!"

A moment later the box was lifted and Philip knew that he was being carried up a step and through a door, then with a suddenness that startled him he found himself standing upright. His prison had been set on end!

"Not that way, man," objected Hodges, for Philip was now certain that he was in the presence of the chief of construction. "Put it down - over there in the corner."

"Not on your life," retorted Fingy, cracking his finger bones fiercely. "See here. Mister Hodges, I ain't a coward, but I b'lieve in bein' to the dead, 'n' to a box that's held one. It says on that red card, 'Head - This end up,' an', s'elp me, it's going to be up, unless you put it down. I ain't goin' to be ha'nted by no ghosts! Ho, ho, ho -" He approached close to the box. "I'll take this red card off, Mister Hodges. It ain't nat'ral when there ain't nothing but maps 'n' things in it."

If the cloth had not been about his mouth, it is possible that Philip would not have restrained audible expression of his astonishment at what happened an instant later. The card was torn off, and a ray of light shot into his eyes. Through a narrow slit not more than a quarter of an inch wide, and six inches long, he found himself staring out into the room. The. Fingy was close behind him. And in the rear of these two, as if eager for their departure, was Hodges, chief of construction. No sooner had the men gone than Hodges turned back to the table in the center of the office. It was not difficult for Philip to see that the man's face was flushed and that he was laboring under some excitement. He sat down, fumbled over some papers, rose quickly to his feet, looked at his watch, and began pacing back and forth across the room.

"So she's coming," he chuckled gleefully.

"She's coming, at last!" He looked at his watch again, straightened his cravat before a mirror, and rubbed his hands with a low laugh. "The little beauty has surrendered," he went on, his face turning for an instant toward the coffin box. "And it's time - past time."

A light knock sounded at the door, and the chief sprang to open it. A figure darted past him, and for but a breath a white, beautiful face was turned toward Philip and his prison - the face of the young woman whom he had seen but two hours before in Le Pas, the face that had pleaded with him that night, that had smiled upon him from the photograph, and that seemed to be masked now in a cold marble-like horror, as its glorious eyes, like pools of glowing fire, seemed searching him out through that narrow slit in the coffin box.

Hodges had advanced, with arms reaching out, and the woman turned with a low, sobbing breath breaking from her lips.

Another step and Hodges would have taken her in his arms, but she evaded him with a quick movement, and pointed to a chair at one side of the table.

"Sit down!" she cried softly. "Sit down, and listen!"

Was it fancy, or did her eyes turn with almost a prayer in them to the box against the wall? Philip's heart was beating like a drum. That one word he knew was intended for him.

"Sit down," she repeated, as Hodges hesitated. "Sit down - there - and I will sit here. Before - before you touch me, I want an understanding. You will let me talk, and listen - listen!"

Again that one word - "listen!"-Philip knew was intended for him.

The chief had dropped into his chair, and his visitor seated herself opposite him, with her face toward Philip. She flung back the fur from about her shoulders, and took off her fur turban, so that the light of the big hanging lamp fell full upon the glory of her hair, and set off more vividly the ivory pallor of her cheeks, in which a short time before Philip had seen the rich crimson glow of life, and something that was not fear.

"We must come to an understanding," she repeated, fixing her eyes steadily upon the man before her. "I would sacrifice my life for him - for my husband - and you are demanding that I do more than that. I must be sure of the reward!"

Hodges leaned forward eagerly, as if about to speak, but she interrupted him.

"Listen!" she cried, a fire beginning to burn through the whiteness of her cheeks. "It was you who urged him to come up here when, through misfortune, we lost our little home down in Marion. You offered him work, and he accepted it, believing you a friend. He still thought you a friend when I knew that you were a traitor, planning and scheming to wreck his life, and mine. He would not listen when I spoke to him, without arousing his suspicions, of my abhorrence of you. He trusted you. He was ready to fight for you. And you - you -"

In her excitement the young woman's hands gripped the edges of the table. For a few moments her breath seemed to choke her, and then she continued, her voice trembling with passion.

"And you - you followed me about like a serpent, making every hour of my life one of misery, because he believed in

James Oliver Curwood

you, and I dared not tell him. So I kept it from him - until that night you came to our cabin when he was away, and dared to take me in your arms, to kiss me, and I - I told him then, and he hunted you down and would have killed you if there hadn't been others near to give you help. My God, I love him more because of that! But I was wrong. I should have killed you!"

She stopped, her breath breaking in a sob.

With a sudden movement Hodges sprang from his chair and came toward her, his face flushed, his lips smiling; but, quicker than he, Thorpe's wife was upon her feet, and from his prison Philip saw the rapid rising and falling of her bosom, the threatening fire in her beautiful eyes as she faced him.

"Ah, but you are beautiful!" he heard the man say.

With a cry, in which there was mingled all the passion and gloating joy of triumph, Hodges caught her in his arms. In that moment every vein in Philip's body seemed flooded with fire. He saw the woman's face again, now tense and white in an agony of terror, saw her struggle to free herself, heard the smothered cry that fell from her lips. For the first time he strained to free himself, to cry out through the thick bandage that gagged him. The box trembled. His mightiest effort almost sent it crashing to the floor. Sweating, powerless, he looked again through the narrow slit. In the struggle the woman's hair had loosened, and tumbled now in shining masses down her back. Her hands were gripping at Hodges' throat. Then one of them crept down to her bosom, and with that movement there came a terrible, muffled report. With a groan the chief staggered back and sank to the floor.

For a moment, stupefied by what she had done, Thorpe's wife stood with smoking pistol in her hand, gazing upon the still form at her feet. Then, slowly, like one facing a terrible accuser, she turned straight to the coffin box. The weapon that she held fell to the floor. Without a tremor in her beautiful face she went to one side of the room, picked up a small belt-ax, and began prying off the cover to Philip's prison. There was still no hesitation, no tremble of fear in her face or hands when the cover gave way and Philip stood revealed, his face as white as her own and bathed in a perspiration of excitement and horror. Calmly she took away the cloth about his mouth, loosened the straps about his legs and arms and body, and then she stood back, still speechless, her hands clutching at her bosom while she waited for him to step forth.

His first movement was to fall upon his knees beside Hodges. He bowed his head, listened, and held his hand under the man's waistcoat. Then he looked up. The woman was bending over him, her eyes meeting his own unflinchingly.

"He is dead!" he said quietly.

"Yes, my brother, he is dead!"

The sweet, low tones of the woman's voice rose scarcely above a whisper. The meaning of her words sank into his very soul.

"My sister -" he repeated, hardly knowing that the words were on his lips. "My -"

"Or - your wife," she interrupted, and her hand rested gently for a moment upon his shoulder. "Or your wife - what would you have had her do?"

Her voice - the gentleness of her touch, sent his mind flashing back to that other tragic moment in a little cabin far north, when he had almost killed a man, and for less than this that he had heard and seen. It seemed, for an instant, as though the voice so near to him was coming, faintly, pleadingly, from that other woman at Lac Bain - the woman who had almost caused a tragedy similar to this, only with the sexes changed. He would have excused Colonel Becker for killing Bucky Nome, for defending his own honor and his wife's. And here - now - was a woman who had fought and killed for her own honor, and to save her husband. His sister - his wife - Would he have had them do this? Would he have Mrs. Becker, the woman he loved, defend her honor as this woman had defended hers? Would he not have loved her ten times - a hundred times - more for doing so?

He rose to his feet, making an effort to steel himself against the justice of what he had seen - against the glory of love, of womanhood, of triumph which he saw shining in her eyes.

"I understand now," he said. "You had me brought here - in this way - that I might hear what was said, and use it as evidence. But -"

"Oh, my God, I did not mean to do this," she cried, as if knowing what he was about to say. "I thought that if he betrayed his vileness to you - if he knew that the world would know, through you, how he had attempted to destroy a home, and how he offered my husband's freedom in exchange for - but you saw, you heard, you must understand! He would not dare to go on when he knew that all this would become public. My husband would have been free. But now -"

"You have killed him," said Philip.

There was no sympathy in his voice. It was the cold, passionless accusation of a man of the law, and the woman bowed her face in her hands. He put on his service cap, tightened his belt, and touched her gently on the arm.

"Do you know where your husband is confined?" he asked. "I will take you there, and you may remain with him to-night."

She brightened instantly. "Yes," she said.

"Come!"

They passed through the door, closing it carefully behind them, and the woman led the way to a dark, windowless building a hundred yards from the dead chief's headquarters.

"This is the camp prison," she whispered.

A man clad in a great bear-skin coat was on guard at the door. In the moonlight he recognized Philip's uniform.

"Here are orders from the inspector," said Philip, holding out MacGregor's letter. "I am to have charge of the prisoner. Mrs. Thorpe is to spend the night with him."

A moment later the door was opened and the woman passed in. As he turned away Philip heard a low sobbing cry, a man's startled voice. Then the door swung heavily on its hinges and there was silence.

Five minutes later Philip was bending again over the dead man. A surprising transformation had come over him now. His face was flushed and his strong teeth shone in sneering hatred as he covered the body with a blanket. On the wall hung a pair of overalls and a working-man's heavy coat. These and Hodges' hat he quickly put on in place of his own uniform. Once more he went out into the night.

This time he came up back of the prison. The guard was pacing back and forth in his beaten path, so thickly muffled about the ears that he did not hear Philip's cautious footsteps behind him. When he turned he found the muzzle of a revolver within arm's length of his face.

"Hands up!" commanded Philip.

The astonished man obeyed without a word.

"If you make a move or the slightest sound I'll kill you!" continued Philip threateningly. "Drop your hands behind you - there, like that!"

With the quickness and skill which he had acquired under Sergeant Moody he secured the guard's wrists with one of the coffin box straps, and gagged him with the same cloth that had been used upon himself. He had observed that his prisoner carried the key to the padlocked cabin in one of his coat pockets, and after possessing himself of this he made him seat himself in the deep shadow, strapped his ankles, and then unlocked the prison door.

There was a light inside, and from beyond this the white faces of the man and the woman stared at him as he entered. The man was leaning back in his cot, and Philip knew that the wife had risen suddenly, for one arm was still encircling his shoulders, and a hand was resting on his cheek as if she had been stroking it caressingly when he interrupted them. Her beautiful, startled eyes gazed at him half defiantly now.

He advanced into the light, took off his hat, and smiled.

With a cry Thorpe's wife sprang to her feet.

"Sh-h-h-h-h!" warned Philip, raising a hand and pointing to the door behind them.

Thorpe had risen. Without a word Philip advanced and held out his hand. Only half understanding, the prisoner reached forth his own. As, for an instant, the two men stood in this position, one smiling, the other transfixed with wonder, there came a stifled, sobbing cry from behind. Philip turned. The woman stood in the lamp glow, her arms reaching out to him - to both - and never, not even at Lac Bain, had he seen a woman more beautiful than Thorpe's wife at that moment.

As if nothing had happened, he went to the table, where there was a pen and ink and a pad of paper.

"Perhaps your wife hasn't told you everything that has happened to-night, Thorpe," he said. "If she hasn't, she will - soon. Now, listen!"

He had pulled a small book from an inner pocket and was writing.

"My name is Steele, Philip Steele, of the Royal Mounted. Down in Chicago I've got a father, Philip Egbert Steele, a banker, who's worth half a dozen millions or so. You're going down to him as fast as dog-sledge and train can carry you, and you'll give him this note. It says that your name is Johnson, and that for my sake he's going to put you on your feet, so that it is going to be pretty blamed comfortable for yourself - and the noblest little woman I've ever met. Do you understand, Thorpe?"

He looked up. Thorpe's wife had gone to her husband. She stood now, half in his arms, and looking at him; as they were, they reminded him of a couple who had played the finale in a drama which he had seen a year before.

"There is one favor which you must do me, Thorpe," he went on. "At home I am rich. Up here I'm only Phil Steele, of the Royal Mounted. I'm telling you so that you won't think that I'm stripping myself when I make you take this. It's a little ready cash, and a check for a thousand dollars. Some day, if you want to, you can pay it back. Now hustle up and get on your clothes. I imagine that your friends are somewhere near - with the sledge that brought me up from Le Pas. Tomorrow, of course, I shall be compelled to take up the pursuit. But if you hurry I don't believe that I shall catch you."

He rose and put on his hat, leaving the money and the check on the table. The woman staggered toward him, the man following in a dazed, stunned sort of way. He saw the woman's arms reaching out to him again, a look in her beautiful face that he would never forget.

In another moment he had opened the door and was gone.

CHAPTER VIII

ANOTHER LETTER FOR PHILIP

From beside his prisoner in the deep gloom Philip saw Thorpe and his wife come out of the cabin a minute later and hurry away through the night. Then he dragged the guard into the prison, relocked the door, left the key in the lock, and returned to Hodges' office to replace the old clothes for his uniform. Not until he stood looking down upon the dead body again did the enormity of his own offense begin to crowd upon him. But he was not frightened nor did he regret what he had done. He turned out the light, sat down, coolly filled his pipe, and began turning the affair over, detail by detail, in his mind. He had, at least, followed Inspector MacGregor's injunction - he had followed his conscience. Hodges had got what he deserved, and he had saved a man and a woman.

But in spite of his first argument, he knew that MacGregor had not foreseen a tragedy of this sort, and that, in the eyes of the law, he was guilty of actively assisting in the flight of two people who could not possibly escape the penalty of justice - if caught. But they would not be caught. He assured himself of that, smiling grimly in the darkness. No one at Wekusko could explain what had happened.

He was positive that the guard had not recognized him, and that he would think one of Thorpe's friends had effected the rescue. And MacGregor - Philip chuckled as he thought of the condemning evidence in his possession, the strange orders which would mean dismissal for the inspector, and perhaps a greater punishment, if he divulged them. He would be safe in telling MacGregor something of what had occurred in the little cabin. And then, as he sat in this grim atmosphere of death, a thought came to him of M'sieur Janette's skull, of Bucky Nome, and of the beautiful young wife at Lac Bain.

If Mrs. Becker could know of this, too - if Bucky Nome, buried somewhere deep in the northern wilderness, could only see Hodges as he lay there, dead on the cabin floor! To the one it would be a still greater punishment, to the other a warning. And yet, even as he thought of the colonel's wife and of her flirtation with Nome, a vision of her face came to him again, filled with the marvelous sweetness, the purity, and the love which had enthralled him beside the campfire. In these moments it was almost impossible for him to convince himself that she had forgotten her dignity as a wife even for an hour. Could he have been mistaken? Had he looked at her with eyes heated by his own love, fired by jealousy? If she had smiled upon him instead of upon Bucky Nome, if her cheeks had flushed at his words, would he have thought that she had done wrong? As if in answer to his own questions, he saw again the white, tense face of the colonel, her husband, and he laughed harshly.

For several hours Philip remained in the shelter of Hodges' office. With early dawn he stole out into the forest, and a little later made his appearance in camp, saying that he had spent the night at Le Pas. Not until an hour later was it discovered that Hodges had been killed, the guard made a prisoner, and that Thorpe and his wife were gone. Philip at once took charge of affairs and put a strain on his professional knowledge by declaring that Thorpe had undoubtedly fled into the North. Early in the afternoon he started in pursuit.

A dozen miles north of the Wekusko camp he swung at right angles to the west, traveled fifteen miles, then cut a straight course south. It was three days later before he showed up at Le Pas, and learned that no one had seen or heard of Thorpe and his wife. Two days later he walked into MacGregor's office. The inspector fairly leaped from his chair to greet him.

"You got them, Steele!" he cried. "You got them after the mur - the killing of Hodges?"

Philip handed him a crumpled bit of paper.

"Those were your latest instructions, sir," he replied quietly. "I followed them to the letter."

MacGregor read, and his face turned as white as the paper he held. "Good God!" he gasped.

He reeled rather than walked back to his desk, dropped into a chair and buried his face in his arms, his shoulders shaking like those of a sobbing boy. It was a long time before he looked up, and during these minutes Philip, with his head bowed low to the other, told him of all that had happened in the little room at Wekusko. But he did not say that it was he who had surprised the guard and released Thorpe and his wife.

At last MacGregor raised his head.

"Philip," he said, taking the young man's hand in both his own, "since she was a little girl and I a big, strapping playmate of nineteen, I have loved her. She is the only girl - the only woman - I have ever loved. You understand? I am almost old enough to be her father. She was never intended for me. But things like this happen - sometimes, and when she came to plead with me the other day I almost yielded. That is why I chose you, warned you -"

He stopped, and a sob rose in his breast.

"And at last you did yield," said Philip.

The inspector gazed at him for a moment in silence. Then he said: "It was ten years ago, on her seventeenth birthday, that I made her a present of a little silver-bound autograph book, and on the first page of that book I wrote the words which saved her husband - and her. Do you understand now, Philip? It was her last card, and she played it well."

He smiled faintly, and then said, as if to no one but himself, "God bless her!"

He looked down on the big, tawny head that was bowed again upon the desk, and placed his hands on the other's shoulders.

"God bless her!" echoed Philip.

"You are not alone in your sorrows, Felix MacGregor," he said softly. "You asked me if I was beauty-proof. Yes, I am. And it is because of something like this, because of a face and a soul that have filled my heart, because of a woman that is not mine, and never can be mine, because of a love which ever burns, and must never be known - it is because of this that I am beauty-proof. God bless this little woman, MacGregor - and you - and I - will never ask where she has gone."

MacGregor's hand reached out and gripped his own in silence. In that hand-clasp there was sealed a pact between them, and Philip returned to his barracks room to write a letter, in care of his father, to the man and woman whom he had helped to escape into the south. He spent the greater part of that day writing. It was late in the afternoon that Moody came in with the mail.

"One for you, Phil," he said, tossing a letter on Philip's table. "Looks as though it had been through a war."

Philip picked up the letter as the sergeant left him. He dropped his pen with a low whistle. He could see at a glance that the letter had come an unusual journey. It was dirty, and crumpled, and ragged at the ends - and then, on the back of it, he found written in ink, "Lac Bain." His fingers trembled as he tore open the envelope. Swiftly he read. His breath came in a gasping cry from between his lips, his face turned as white as the crumpled paper, and then, as suddenly, a flush of excitement leaped into his cheeks, replacing the pallor. His eyes seemed blinded before he had half finished the letter, and his heart was pounding with suffocating force.

This was what he read:

My Dear Philip Steele:

Your letter, and the skull, came to us to-day. I thank God that chance brought me into my Isobel's room in time, or I fear for what might have happened. It was a terrible punishment, my dear Steele, for her - and for me. But I deserved it more than she. That very night - after Isobel left the table - she insisted that I explain. When I returned to the room below, you were gone. I waited, and then went to your cabin. You know why I did not find you. Steele, Isobel is not my wife. She is my daughter.

Mrs. Becker had planned to come with me to Lac Bain from Fort Churchill, and we wrote the factor to that effect. But we changed our plans. Mrs. Becker returned on the London ship, and Isobel came with me. In a spirit of fun she suggested that for the first few hours she be allowed to pass as - well, you understand. The joke was carried too far. When she met you - and Bucky Nome - it ceased to be a joke, and almost became a tragedy. For those few minutes before the fire Isobel used her disguise as a test. She came to me, before you joined us, and whispered to me that Nome was a scoundrel, and that she would punish him before the evening was over. In the short space of that evening she knew that she had met one of the most despicable of blackguards in Nome, and one of the noblest of men in you. And not until she saw on you the effect of what she was doing did everything dawn fully upon her.

You know what happened. She left the table suddenly, overcome by shame and terror. When I returned later, and told her that I could not find you, it was impossible to comfort her.

She lay in her bed crying all that night. I am telling you all this, because to me my daughter is one of the two most precious things on earth, the sweetest and purest little girl that ever breathed. I can not describe to you the effect upon her of the skull and the letter. Forgive us - forgive me. Some day we may meet again

Sylvester Becker.

Like one in a dream Philip picked up the torn envelope. Something dropped from it upon the table - a tiny cluster of violets that had been pressed and dried between the pages of a book, and when he took them in his fingers, he found that their stems were tied with a single thread of golden hair!

CHAPTER IX

PHILIP TAKES UP THE TRAIL

The letter - the flowers - that one shining golden hair, wound in a glistening thread about their shriveled stems, seemed for a short space to lift Philip Steele from out of the world he was in, to another in which his mind was only vaguely conscious, stunned by this letter that had come with the unexpectedness of a thunderbolt to change, in a single instant, every current of life in his body. For a few moments he made no effort to grasp the individual significance of the letter, the flowers, the golden hair. One thought filled his brain - one great, overpowering truth, which excluded everything else - and this was the realization that the woman he loved was not Colonel Becker's wife. She was free. And for him - Philip Steele - there was hope - hope - Suddenly it dawned upon him what the flowers meant. The colonel had written the letter, and Isobel had sent the faded violets, with their golden thread. It was her message to him - a message without words, and yet with a deeper meaning for him than words could have expressed. In a flood there rushed back upon him all the old visions which he had fought against, and he saw her again in the glow of the campfire, and on the trail, glorious in her beauty, his ideal of all that a woman should be.

He rose to his feet and locked his door, fearing that some one might enter. He wanted to be alone, to realize fully what had happened, to regain control of his emotions. If Isobel Becker had merely written him a line or two, a note exculpating herself of what her father had already explained away, he would still have thought that a world lay between them. But, in place of that, she had sent him the faded flowers, with their golden thread!

For many minutes he paced back and forth across his narrow room, and never had a room looked more like a prison cell to him than this one did now. He was filled with but one impulse, and that was to return to Lac Bain, to humble himself at the feet of the woman he loved, and ask her forgiveness for the heinous thing he had done. He wanted to tell her that he had driven Bucky Nome into outlawry, that he had fought for her, and run away himself - because he loved her. It was Sergeant Moody's voice, vibrant with the rasping unpleasantness of a file, that jarred him back into his practical self. He thrust the letter and the flowers into his breast pocket, and opened the door.

Moody came in.

"What in blazes are you locked up for?" he demanded, his keen little eyes scrutinizing Philip's feverish face. "Afraid somebody'll walk in and steal you, Phil?"

"Headache," said Philip, patting a hand to his head. "One of the kind that makes you think your brain must be a hard ball bumping around inside your skull."

The sergeant laid his hand on Philip's arm.

"Go take a walk, Phil," he said, in a softer voice. "It will do you good. I just came in to tell you the news. They've got track of DeBar again, up near Lac la Biche. But we can talk about that later. Go take a walk."

"Thanks for the suggestion," said Philip. "I believe I'll do it."

He passed beyond the barracks, and hit the sleigh-worn road that led out of town, walking faster and faster, as his brain began working. He would return to Lac Bain. That was settled in his mind without argument. Nothing could hold him back after what he had received that afternoon. If the letter and the violet message had come to him from the end of the earth it would have made no difference; his determination would have been the same. He would return to Lac Bain - but how? That was the question which puzzled him. He still had thirteen months of service ahead of him. He was not in line for a furlough. It would take at least three months of official red tape to purchase his discharge. These facts rose like barriers in his way. It occurred to him that he might confide in MacGregor, and that the inspector would make an opportunity for him to return into the north immediately. MacGregor had the power to do that, and he believed that he would do it. But he hesitated to accept this last alternative.

And then, all at once. Sergeant Moody's words came back to him - "They've got track of DeBar again, up near Lac la Biche." The idea that burst upon him with the recalling of those words stopped Philip suddenly, and he turned back toward the barracks. He had heard a great deal about DeBar, the cleverest criminal in all the northland, and whom no man or combination of men had been clever enough to catch. And now this man was near Lac la Biche, in the Churchill and Lac Bain country. It he could get permission from MacGregor to go after DeBar his own difficulty would be settled in the easiest possible way. The assignment would take him for a long and indefinite time into the north. It would take him back to Isobel Becker.

He went immediately to his room upon reaching the barracks, and wrote out his request to MacGregor. He sent it over to headquarters by a rookie. After that he waited.

Not until the following morning did Moody bring him a summons to appear in MacGregor's office. Five minutes later the inspector greeted him with outstretched hand, gave him a grip that made his fingers snap, and locked the office door. He was holding Philip's communication when the young man entered.

"I don't know what to say to this, Steele," he began, seating himself at his desk and motioning Philip to a chair. "To be frank with you, this proposition of yours is entirely against my best judgment."

"In other words, you haven't sufficient confidence in me," added Philip.

"No, I don't mean that. There isn't a man on the force in whom I have greater confidence than you. But, if I was to gamble, I'd wager ten to one that you'd lose out if I sent you up to take this man DeBar."

"I'll accept that wager - only reverse the odds," said Philip daringly.

The inspector twisted one of his long red mustaches and smiled a little grimly at the other.

"If I were to follow my own judgment I'd not send one man, but two," he went on. "I don't mean to underestimate the value of my men when I say that our friend DeBar, who has evaded us for years, is equal to any two men I've got. I wouldn't care to go after him myself - alone. I'd want another hand with me, and a mighty good one - a man who was cool, cautious, and who knew all of the ins and outs of the game as well as myself. And here -" He interrupted himself, and chuckled audibly, "here you are asking permission to go after him alone! Why, man, it's the very next thing to inviting yourself to commit suicide! Now, if I were to send you, and along with you a good, level-headed man like Moody -"

"I have had enough of double-harness work, unless I am commanded to go, Mr. MacGregor," interrupted Philip. "I realize that DeBar is a dangerous man, but I believe that I can bring him down. Will you give me the opportunity?"

James Oliver Curwood

MacGregor laid his cigar on the edge of the desk and leaned across toward his companion, the long white fingers of his big hands clasped in front of him. He always took this position, with a cigar smoldering beside him, when about to say those things which he wished to be indelibly impressed on the memory of his listener.

"Yes, I'm going to give you the opportunity," he said slowly, "and I am also going to give you permission to change your mind after I have told you something about DeBar, whom we know as the Seventh Brother. I repeat that, if you go alone, it's just ten to one that you don't get him. Since '99 four men have gone out after him, and none has come back. There was Forbes, who went in that year; Bannock, who took up the trial in 1902; Fleisham in 1904, and Gresham in 1907. Since the time of Gresham's disappearance we have lost sight of DeBar, and only recently, as you know, have we got trace of him again. He is somewhere up on the edge of the Barren Lands. I have private information which leads me to believe that the factor at Fond du Lac can take you directly to him."

MacGregor unclasped his hands to pick up a worn paper from a small pile on the desk.

"He is the last of seven brothers," he added. "His father was hanged."

"A good beginning," interjected Philip.

"There's just the trouble," said the inspector quickly. "It wasn't a good beginning. This is one of those peculiar cases of outlawry for which the law itself is largely responsible, and I don't know of any one I would say this to but you. The father was hanged, as I have said. Six months later it was discovered, beyond a doubt, that the law had taken the life of an innocent man, and that DeBar had been sent to the gallows by a combination of evidence fabricated entirely by the perjury of enemies. The law should have vindicated itself. But it didn't. Two of those who had plotted against DeBar were arrested, tried - and acquitted, a fact which goes to prove the statement of a certain great man that half of the time law is not justice. There is no need of going into greater detail about the trials and the plled the three men chiefly instrumental in sending their father to his death, and fled into the North."

"Good!" exclaimed Philip.

The word shot from him before he had thought. At first he flushed, then sat bolt upright and smiled frankly into the inspector's face as he watched the effect of his indiscretion.

"So many people thought at the time," said MacGregor, eying him with curious sharpness. "Especially the women. For that reason the first three who were caught were merely convicted of manslaughter instead of murder. They served their sentences, were given two years each for good behavior, and are somewhere in South America. The fourth killed himself when he was taken near Moose Factory, and the other three went what the law calls 'bad.' Henry, the oldest of them all, killed the officer who was bringing him down from Prince Albert in '99, and was afterward executed. Paul, the sixth, returned to his native town seven years after the hanging of his father and was captured after wounding two of the officers who went in pursuit of him. He is now in an insane asylum."

The inspector paused, and ran his eyes over a fresh slip of paper.

"And all this," said Philip in a low voice, "because of a crime committed by the law itself. Five men hung, one a suicide, three in prison and one in an insane asylum - because of a blunder of the law!"

"The king can do no wrong," said MacGregor with gentle irony, "and neither can the law. Remember that, Philip, as long as you are in the service. The law may break up homes, ruin states, set itself a Nemesis on innocent men's heels - but it can do no wrong. It is the Juggernaut before which we all must bow our heads, even you and I, and when by any chance it makes a mistake, it is still law, and unassailable. It is the greatest weapon of the clever and the rich, so it bears a moral. Be clever, or be rich."

"And William DeBar, the seventh brother -" began Philip.

"Is tremendously clever, but not rich," finished the inspector. "He has caused us more trouble than any other man in Canada. He is the youngest of the seven brothers, and you know there are curious superstitions about seventh brothers. In the first pursuit after the private hanging he shot two men. He killed a third in an attempt to save his brother at Moose Factory. Since then, Forbes, Bannock, Fleisham and Gresham have disappeared, and they all went out after him. They were all good men, powerful physically, skilled in the ways of the wilderness, and as brave as tigers. Yet they all failed. And not only that, they lost their lives. Whether DeBar killed them, or led them on to a death for which his hands were not directly responsible, we have never known. The fact remains that they went out after De Bar - and died. I am not superstitious, but I am beginning to think that DeBar is more than a match for any one man. What do you say? Will you go with Moody, or -"

"I'll go alone, with your permission," said Philip.

The inspector's voice at once fell into its formal tone of command.

"Then you may prepare to leave at once," he said. "The factor at Fond du Lac will put you next to your man. Whatever else you require I will give you in writing some time to-day."

Philip accepted this as signifying that the interview was at an end, and rose from his seat.

That night he added a postscript to the letter which he had written home, saying that for a long time he would not be heard from again. The midnight train was bearing him toward Le Pas.

James Oliver Curwood

CHAPTER X

ISOBEL'S DISAPPEARANCE

Four hundred miles as an arrow might fly, five hundred by snowshoes and dog-sledge; up the Pelican Lake waterway, straight north along the edge of the Geikie Barrens, and from Wollaston westward, Philip hurried - not toward the hiding place of William DeBar, but toward Lac Bain.

A sledge and six dogs with a half-breed driver took him from Le Pas as far as the Churchill; with two Crees, on snow-shoes, he struck into the Reindeer country, and two weeks later bought a sledge and three dogs at an Indian camp on the Waterfound. On the second day, in the barrens to the west, one of the dogs slit his foot on a piece of ice; on the third day the two remaining dogs went lame, and Philip and his guide struck camp at the headwater of the Gray Beaver, sixty miles from Lac Bain. It was impossible for the dogs to move the following day, so Philip left his Indian to bring them in later and struck out alone.

That day he traveled nearly thirty miles, over a country broken by timbered ridges, and toward evening came to the beginning of the open country that lay between him and the forests about Lac Bain. It had been a hard day's travel, but he did not feel exhausted. The full moon was rising at nine o'clock, and Philip rested for two hours, cooking and eating his supper, and then resumed his journey, determined to make sufficient progress before camping to enable him to reach the post by the following noon. It was midnight when he put up his light tent, built a fire, and went to sleep. He was up again at dawn. At two o'clock he came into the clearing about Lac Bain. As he hurried to Breed's quarters he wondered if Colonel Becker or Isobel had seen him from their window. He had noticed that the curtain was up, and that a thin spiral of smoke was rising from the clay chimney that descended to the fireplace in their room.

He found Breed, the factor, poring over one of the ledgers which he and Colonel Becker had examined. He started to his feet when he saw Philip.

"Where in the name of blazes have you been?" were his first words, as he held out a hand. "I've been hunting the country over for you, and had about come to the conclusion that you and Bucky Nome were dead."

"Hunting for me," said Philip. "What for?"

Breed shrugged his shoulders.

"The colonel an' - Miss Isobel," he said. "They wanted to see you so bad that I had men out for three days after you'd gone looking for you. Couldn't even find your trail. I'm curious to know what was up."

Philip laughed. He felt a tingling joy running through every vein in his body. It was difficult for him to repress the trembling eagerness in his voice, as he said: "Well, I'm here. I wonder if they want to see me - now."

"Suppose they do," replied Breed, slowly lighting his pipe. "But you've hung off too long. They're gone."

"Gone?" Philip stared at the factor.

"Gone?" he demanded again.

"Left this morning - for Churchill," affirmed Breed. "Two sledges, two Indians, the colonel and Miss Isobel."

For a few moments Philip stood in silence, staring straight out through the one window of the room with his back to the factor.

"Did they leave any word for me?" he asked.

"No."

"Then - I must follow them!" He spoke the words more to himself than to Breed. The factor regarded him in undisguised astonishment and Philip, turning toward him, hastened to add: "I can't tell you why. Breed - but it's necessary that I overtake them as soon as possible. I don't want to lose a day - not an hour. Can you lend me a team and a driver?"

"I've got a scrub team," said Breed, "but there isn't another man that I can spare from the post. There's LeCroix, ten miles to the west. If you can wait until to-morrow -"

"I must follow this afternoon - now," interrupted Philip. "They will have left a clean trail behind, and I can overtake them some time to-morrow. Will you have the team made ready for me - a light sledge, it you've got it."

By three o'clock he was on the trail again. Breed had spoken truthfully when he said that his dogs were scrubs. There were four of them, two mongrels, one blind huskie, and a mamelute that ran lame. And besides this handicap, Philip found that his own endurance was fast reaching the ebbing point. He had traveled sixty miles in a day and a half, and his legs and back began to show signs of the strain. In spite of this fact, his spirits rose with every mile he placed behind him. He knew that it would be impossible for Isobel and her father to stand the hardship of fast and continued travel. At the most they would not make more than twenty miles in a day, and even with his scrub team he could make thirty, and would probably overtake them at the end of the next day. And then it occurred to him, with a pleasurable thrill, that to find Isobel again on the trail, as he had first seen her, would be a hundred times better than finding her at Lac Bain. He would accompany her and the colonel to Churchill. They would be together for days, and at the end of that time -

He laughed low and joyously, and for a spell he urged the dogs into a swifter pace. That he had correctly estimated the speed of those ahead of him he was convinced, when, two hours later, he came upon the remains of their mid-day camp-fire, nine or ten miles from Lac Bain. It was dark when he reached this point. There were glowing embers still in the fire, and these he stirred into life, adding armfuls of dry wood to the flames. About him in the snow he found the prints of Isobel's little feet, and in the flood of joy and hope that was sweeping more and more into his life he sang and whistled, and forgot that he was alone in a desolation of blackness that made even the dogs slink nearer to the fire. He would camp here - where Isobel had been only a few hours before. If he traveled hard he would overtake them by the next noon.

But he had underestimated his own exhaustion. After he had put up his tent before the fire he made himself a bed of balsam boughs and fell into a deep sleep, from which neither dawn nor the restless movements of the dogs could awaken him. When at last he opened his eyes it was broad day. He jumped to his feet and looked at his watch. It was nine o'clock, and after ten before he again took up the pursuit of the two sledges. Not until several hours later did he give up hope of overtaking Isobel and her father as he had planned, and he reproved himself roundly for having overslept. The afternoon was half gone before he struck their camp of the preceding evening, and he knew that, because of his own loss of time, Isobel was still as far ahead of him as when he had left Lac Bain.

He made up some of this time by following the trail for an hour when the moon was at its highest, and then pitched his tent. He was up again the next morning and breaking camp

James Oliver Curwood

before it was light. Scarcely had he traveled an hour over the clear-cut trail ahead of him when he suddenly halted his dogs with a loud cry of command and astonishment. In a small open the trails of the two sledges separated. One continued straight east, toward Churchill, while the other turned almost at right angles into the south. For a few moments he could find no explanation for this occurrence. Then he decided that one of the Indians had struck southward, either to hunt, or on some short mission, and that he would join the other sledge farther on. Convinced that this was the right solution, Philip continued over the Churchill trail. A little later, to his despair, it began to snow so heavily that the trail which he was following was quickly obliterated. There was but one thing for him to do now, and that was to hasten on to Fort Churchill, giving up all hope of finding Isobel and the colonel before he met them there.

Four days later he came into the post. The news that awaited him struck him dumb. Isobel and her father, with one Indian, had gone with the sledge into the South. The Indian who had driven on to Churchill could give no further information, except that he knew the colonel and his daughter had suddenly changed their minds about coming to Churchill. Perhaps they had gone to Nelson House, or York Factory - or even to Le Pas. He did not know.

It was with a heavy heart that Philip turned his face once more toward Lac Bain. He could not repress a laugh, bitter and filled with disappointment, as he thought how fate was playing against him. If he had not overslept he would have caught up with the sledges before they separated, if he had not forced himself into this assignment it was possible that Isobel and her father would have come to him. They knew that his detachment was at Prince Albert - and they were going south. He had little doubt but that they were striking for Nelson House, and from Nelson House to civilization there was but one trail, that which led to Le Pas and Etomami. And Etomami was but two hours by rail from Prince Albert.

He carried in his breast pocket a bit of written information which he had obtained from the Churchill factor - that helped to soften, in a way, the sting of his disappointment. It was Colonel Becker's London address - and Isobel's, and he quickly laid out for himself new plans of action. He would write to MacGregor from Lac Bain, asking him to put in at once the necessary application for the purchase of his release from the service. As soon as he was free he would go to London. He would call on Isobel like a gentleman, he told himself. Perhaps, after all, it would be the better way.

But first, there was DeBar.

As he had been feverishly anxious to return into the North, so, now, he was anxious to have this affair with DeBar over with. He lost no time at Lac Bain, writing his letter to Inspector MacGregor on the same day that he arrived. Only two of the dogs which the Indian had brought into the post were fit to travel, and with these, and a light sledge on which he packed his equipment he set off alone for Fond du Lac. A week later he reached the post. He found Hutt, the factor, abed with a sprained knee, and the only other men at the post were three Chippewayans, who could neither talk nor understand English.

"DeBar is gone," groaned Hutt, after Philip had made himself known. "A rascal of a Frenchman came in last night on his way to the Grand Rapid, and this morning DeBar was missing. I had the Chippewayans in, and they say he left early in the night with his sledge and one big bull of a hound that he hangs to like grim death. I'd kill that damned Indian you came up with. I believe it was he that told the Frenchman there was an officer on the way."

"Is the Frenchman here?" asked Philip.

"Gone!" groaned Hutt again, turning his twisted knee. "He left for the Grand Rapid this morning, and there isn't another dog or sledge at the post. This winter has been death on the dogs, and what few are left are out on the trap-lines. DeBar knows you're after him, sure as fate, and he's taken a trail toward the Athabasca. The best I can do is to let you have a Chippewayan who'll go with you as far as the Chariot. That's the end of his territory, and what you'll do after that God only knows."

"I'll take the chance," said Philip. "We'll start after dinner. I've got two dogs, a little lame, but even at that they'll have DeBar's outfit handicapped."

It was less than two hours later when Philip and the Chippewayan set off into the western forests, the Indian ahead and Philip behind, with the dogs and sledge between them. Both men were traveling light. Philip had even strapped his carbine and small emergency bag to the toboggan, and carried only his service revolver at his belt. It was one o'clock and the last slanting beams of the winter sun, heatless and only cheering to the eye, were fast dying away before the first dull gray approach of desolate gloom which precedes for a few hours the northern night. As the black forest grew more and more somber about them, he looked over the grayish yellow back of the tugging huskies at the silent Indian striding over the outlaw's trail, and a slight shiver passed through him, a shiver that was neither of cold nor fear, yet which was accompanied by an oppression which it was hard for him to shake off. Deep down in his heart Philip had painted a picture of William DeBar - of the man - and it was a picture to his liking. Such men he would like to know and to call his friends. But now the deepening gloom, the darkening of the sky above, the gray picture ahead of him - the Chippewayan, as silent as the trees, the dogs pulling noiselessly in their traces like slinking shadows, the ghost-like desolation about him, all recalled him to that other factor in the game, who was DeBar the outlaw, and not DeBar the man. In this same way, he imagined, Forbes, Bannock, Fleisham and Gresham had begun the game, and they had lost. Perhaps they, too, had gone out weakened by visions of the equity of things, for the sympathy of man for man is strong when they meet above the sixtieth.

DeBar was ahead of him - DeBar the outlaw, watching and scheming as he had watched and schemed when the other four had played against him. The game had grown old to him. It had brought him victim after victim, and each victim had made of him a more deadly enemy of the next. Perhaps at this moment he was not very far ahead, waiting to send him the way of the others. The thought urged new fire into Philip's blood. He spurted past the dogs and stopped the Chippewayan, and then examined the trail. It was old. The frost had hardened in the huge footprints of DeBar's big hound; it had built a webby film over the square impressions of his snow-shoe thongs. But what of that? Might not the trail still be old, and DeBar a few hundred yards ahead of him, waiting - watching?

He went back to the sledge and unstrapped his carbine. In a moment the first picture, the first sympathy, was gone. It was not the law which DeBar was fighting now. It was himself. He walked ahead of the Indian, alert, listening and prepared. The crackling of a frost-bitten tree startled him into stopping; the snapping of a twig under its weight of ice and snow sent strange thrills through him which left him almost sweating. The sounds were repeated again and again as they advanced, until he became accustomed to them. Yet at each new sound his fingers gripped tighter about his carbine and his heart beat a little faster. Once or twice he spoke to the Indian, who understood no word he said and remained silent. They built a fire and cooked their supper when it grew too dark to travel.

Later, when it became lighter, they went on hour after hour, through the night. At dawn the trail was still old. There were the same cobwebs of frost, the same signs to show that DeBar and his Mackenzie hound had preceded them a long time before. During the next day and night they spent sixteen hours on their snow-shoes and the lacework of frost in DeBar's trail grew thinner. The next day they traveled fourteen and the next twelve, and there was no lacework of frost at all. There were hot coals under the ashes of DeBar's fires. The crumbs of his bannock were soft. The toes of his Mackenzie hound left warm, sharp imprints. It was then that they came to the frozen water of the Chariot. The Chippewayan turned back to Fond du Lac, and Philip went on alone, the two dogs limping behind him with his outfit.

It was still early in the day when Philip crossed the river into the barrens and with each step now his pulse beat faster. DeBar could not be far ahead of him. He was sure of that. Very soon he must overtake him. And then - there would be a fight. In the tense minutes that followed, the vision of Isobel's beautiful face grew less and less distinct in his mind. It was filled with something more grim, something that tightened his muscles, kept him ceaselessly alert. He would come on DeBar - and there would be a fight. DeBar would not be taken by surprise.

At noon he halted and built a small fire between two rocks, over which he boiled some tea and warmed his meat. Each day he had built three fires, but at the end of this day, when darkness stopped him again, it occurred to him that since that morning DeBar had built but one. Gray dawn had scarcely broken when he again took up the pursuit. It was bitterly cold, and a biting wind swept down across the barrens from the Arctic icebergs. His pocket thermometer registered sixty degrees below zero when he left it open on the sledge, and six times between dawn and dusk he built himself fires. Again DeBar built but one, and this time he found no bannock crumbs.

For the last twenty miles DeBar had gone straight into the North. He continued straight into the North the next day and several times Philip scrutinized his map, which told him in that direction there lay nothing but peopleless barrens as far as the Great Slave.

There was growing in him now a fear - a fear that DeBar would beat him out in the race. His limbs began to ache with a strange pain and his progress was becoming slower. At intervals he stopped to rest, and after each of these intervals the pain seemed to gnaw deeper at his bones, forcing him to limp, as the dogs were limping behind him. He had felt it once before, beyond Lac Bain, and knew what it meant. His legs were giving out - and DeBar would beat him yet! The thought stirred him on, and before he stopped again he came to the edge of a little lake. DeBar had started to cross the lake, and then, changing his mind, had turned back and skirted the edge of it. Philip followed the outlaw's trail with his eyes and saw that he could strike it again and save distance by crossing the snow-covered ice.

He went on, with dogs and sledge at his heels, unconscious of the warning underfoot that had turned DeBar back. In midlake he turned to urge the dogs into a faster pace, and it was then that he heard under him a hollow, trembling sound, growing in volume even as he hesitated, until it surged in under his feet from every shore, like the rolling thunder of a ten-pin ball. With a loud cry to the dogs he darted forward, but it was too late. Behind him the ice crashed like brittle glass, and he saw sledge and dogs disappear as if into an abyss. In an instant he had begun a mad race to the shore a hundred feet ahead of him. Ten paces more and he would have reached it, when the toe of his snow-shoe caught in a hummock of snow and ice. For a flash it stopped him, and the moment's pause was fatal. Before he could throw himself forward on his face in a last effort to save himself, the ice gave way and he plunged through. In his extremity he thought of DeBar, of possible help even from the outlaw, and a terrible cry for that help burst from his lips as he felt himself going. The next instant he was sorry that he had shouted. He was to his waist in water, but his feet were on bottom. He saw now what had happened, that the surface of the water was a foot below the shell of ice, which was scarcely more than an inch in thickness. It was not difficult for him to kick off his snow-shoes under the water, and he began breaking his way ashore.

Five minutes later he dragged himself out, stiff with the cold, his drenched clothing freezing as it came into contact with the air. His first thought was of fire, and he ran up the shore, his teeth chattering, and began tearing off handfuls of bark from a birch. Not until he was done and the bark was piled in a heap beside the tree did the full horror of his situation dawn upon him. His emergency pouch was on the sledge, and in that pouch was his waterproof box of matches!

He ran back to the edge of broken ice, unconscious that he was almost sobbing in his despair. There was no sign of the sledge, no sound of the dogs, who might still be struggling in their traces. They were gone - everything - food, fire, life itself. He dug out his flint and steel from the bottom of a stiffening pocket and knelt beside the bark, striking them again and again, yet knowing that his efforts were futile. He continued to strike until his hands were purple and numb and his freezing clothes almost shackled him to the ground.

"Good God!" he breathed.

He rose slowly, with a long, shuddering breath and turned his eyes to where the outlaw's trail swung from the lake into the North. Even in that moment, as the blood in his veins seemed congealing with the icy chill of death, the irony of the situation was not lost upon Philip.

"It's the law versus God, Billy," he chattered, as if DeBar stood before him. "The law wouldn't vindicate itself back there - ten years ago - but I guess it's doing it now."

He dropped into DeBar's trail and began to trot.

"At least it looks as if you're on the side of the Mighty," he continued. "But we'll see - very soon - Billy -"

Ahead of him the trail ran up a ridge, broken and scattered with rocks and stunted scrub, and the sight of it gave him a little hope. Hope died when he reached the top and stared out over a mile of lifeless barren.

"You're my only chance. Billy," he shivered. "Mebby, if you knew what had happened, you'd turn back and give me the loan of a match."

He tried to laugh at his own little joke, but it was a ghastly attempt and his purpling lips closed tightly as he stumbled down the ridge. As his legs grew weaker and his blood more sluggish, his mind seemed to work faster, and the multitude of thoughts that surged through his brain made him oblivious of the first gnawing of a strange dull pain. He was freezing. He knew that without feeling pain. He had before him, not hours, but minutes of life, and he knew that, too. His arms might have been cut off at the shoulders for all feeling that was left in them; he noticed, as he stumbled along in a half run, that he could not bend his fingers. At every step his legs grew heavier and his feet were now leaden weights. Yet he was surprised to find that the first horror of his situation had left him. It did not seem that death was only a few hundred yards away, and he found himself thinking of MacGregor, of home, and then only of Isobel. He wondered, after that, if some one of the other four had played the game, and lost, in this same way, and he wondered, too, if his bones would never be found, as theirs had never been.

He stopped again on a snow ridge. He had come a quarter of a mile, though it seemed that he had traveled ten times that distance.

"Sixty degrees below zero - and it's the vindication of the law!"

His voice scarcely broke between his purple lips now, and the bitter sweep of wind swayed him as he stood.

CHAPTER XI

THE LAW VERSUS THE MAN

Suddenly a great thrill shot through Philip, and for an instant he stood rigid. What was that he saw out in the gray gloom of Arctic desolation, creeping up, up, up, almost black at its beginning, and dying away like a ghostly winding-sheet? A gurgling cry rose in his throat, and he went on, panting now like a broken-winded beast in his excitement. It grew near, blacker, warmer. He fancied that he could feel its heat, which was the new fire of life blazing within him.

He went down between two great drifts into a pit which seemed bottomless. He crawled to the top of the second, using his pulseless hands like sticks in the snow, and at the top something rose from the other side of the drift to meet him.

It was a face, a fierce, bearded face, the gaunt starvation in it hidden by his own blindness. It seemed like the face of an ogre, terrible, threatening, and he knew that it was the face of William DeBar, the seventh brother.

He launched himself forward, and the other launched himself forward, and they met in a struggle which was pathetic in its weakness, and rolled together to the bottom of the drift. Yet the struggle was no less terrible because of that weakness. It was a struggle between two lingering sparks of human life and when these two sparks had flickered and blazed and died down, the two men lay gasping, an arm's reach from each other.

Philip's eyes went to the fire. It was a small fire, burning more brightly as he looked, and he longed to throw himself upon it so that the flames might eat into his flesh. He had mumbled something about police, arrest and murder during the struggle, but DeBar spoke for the first time now.

"You're cold," he said.

"I'm freezing to death," said Philip.

"And I'm - starving."

DeBar rose to his feet. Philip drew himself together, as if expecting an attack, but in place of it DeBar held out a warmly mittened hand.

"You've got to get those clothes off - quick - or you'll die," he said. "Here!"

Mechanically Philip reached up his hand, and DeBar took him to his sledge behind the fire and wrapped about him a thick blanket. Then he drew out a sheath knife and ripped the frozen legs of his trousers up and the sleeves of his coat down, cut the string of his shoe-packs and slit his heavy German socks, and after that he rubbed his feet and legs and arms until Philip began to feel a sting like the prickly bite of nettles.

"Ten minutes more and you'd been gone," said DeBar.

He wrapped a second blanket around Philip, and dragged the sledge on which he was lying still nearer to the fire. Then he threw on a fresh armful of dry sticks and from a pocket of his coat drew forth something small and red and frozen, which was the carcass of a bird about the size of a robin. DeBar held it up between his forefinger and thumb, and looking at Philip, the flash of a smile passed for an instant over his grizzled face.

"Dinner," he said, and Philip could not fail to catch the low chuckling note of humor in his voice. "It's a Whisky Jack, man, an' he's the first and last living thing I've seen in the way of fowl between here and Fond du Lac. He weighs four ounces if he weighs an ounce, and we'll feast on him shortly. I haven't had a full mouth of grub since day before yesterday morning, but you're welcome to a half of him, if you're hungry enough."

"Where'd your chuck go?" asked Philip.

He was conscious of a new warmth and comfort in his veins, but it was not this that sent a heat into his face at the outlaw's offer. DeBar had saved his life, and now, when DeBar might have killed him, he was offering him food. The man was spitting the bird on the sharpened end of a stick, and when he had done this he pointed to the big Mackenzie hound, tied to the broken stub of a dead sapling.

"I brought enough bannock to carry me to Chippewayan, but he got into it the first night, and what he left was crumbs. You lost yours in the lake, eh?"

"Dogs and everything," said Philip. "Even matches."

"Those ice-traps are bad," said DeBar companionably, slowly turning the bird. "You always want to test the lakes in this country. Most of 'em come from bog springs, and after they freeze, the water drops. Guess you'd had me pretty soon if it hadn't been for the lake, wouldn't you?"

He grinned, and to his own astonishment Philip grinned.

"I was tight after you, Bill."

"Ho! ho! ho!" laughed the outlaw. "That sounds good! I've gone by another name, of course, and that's the first time I've heard my own since -"

He stopped suddenly, and the laugh left his voice and face.

"It sounds - homelike," he added more gently. "What's yours, pardner?"

"Steele - Philip Steele, of the R.N.W.M.P.," said Philip.

"Used to know a Steele once," went on DeBar. "That was back - where it happened. He was one of my friends."

For a moment he turned his eyes on Philip. They were deep gray eyes, set well apart in a face that among a hundred others Philip would have picked out for its frankness and courage. He knew that the man before him was not much more than his own age, yet he appeared ten years older.

He sat up on his sledge as DeBar left his bird to thrust sticks into the snow, on the ends of which he hung Philip's frozen garments close to the fire. From the man Philip's eyes traveled to the dog. The hound yawned in the heat and he saw that one of his fangs was gone.

"If you're starving, why don't you kill the dog?" he asked.

DeBar turned quickly, his white teeth gleaming through his beard.

"Because he's the best friend I've got on earth, or next to the best," he said warmly. "He's stuck to me through thick and thin for ten years. He starved with me, and fought with me, and half died with me, and he's going to live with me as long as I live. Would you eat the flesh of your brother, Steele? He's my brother - the last that your glorious law has left to me. Would you kill him if you were me?"

Something stuck hard and fast in Philip's throat, and he made no reply. DeBar came toward him with the hot bird on the end of his stick. With his knife the outlaw cut the bird into two equal parts, and one of these parts he cut into quarters. One of the smaller pieces he tossed to the hound, who devoured it at a gulp. The half he stuck on the end of his knife and offered to his companion.

"No," said Philip. "I can't."

The eyes of the two men met, and DeBar, on his knees, slowly settled back, still gazing at the," said DeBar, after a moment, "don't be a fool, Steele. Let's forget, for a little while. God knows what's going to happen to both of us to-morrow or next day, and it'll be easier to die with company than alone, won't it? Let's forget that you're the Law and I'm the Man, and that I've killed one or two. We're both in the same boat, and we might as well be a little bit friendly for a few hours, and shake hands, and be at peace when the last minute comes. If we get out of this, and find grub, we'll fight fair and square, and the best man wins. Be square with me, old man, and I'll be square with you, s'elp me God!"

He reached out a hand, gnarled, knotted, covered with callouses and scars, and with a strange sound in his throat Philip caught it tightly in his own.

"I'll be square. Bill!" he cried. "I swear that I'll be square - on those conditions. If we find grub, and live, we'll fight it out - alone - and the best man wins. But I've had food today, and you're starving. Eat that and I'll still be in better condition than you. Eat it, and we'll smoke. Praise God I've got my pipe and tobacco!"

They settled back close in the lee of the drift, and the wind swirled white clouds of snow-mist over their heads, while DeBar ate his bird and Philip smoked. The food that went down DeBar's throat was only a morsel, but it put new life into him, and he gathered fresh armfuls of sticks and sapling boughs until the fire burned Philip's face and his drying clothes sent up clouds of steam. Once, a hundred yards out in the plain, Philip heard the outlaw burst into a snatch of wild forest song as he pulled down a dead stub.

"Seems good to have comp'ny," he said, when he came back

with his load. "My God, do you know I've never felt quite like this - so easy and happy like, since years and years? I wonder if it is because I know the end is near?"

"There's still hope," replied Philip.

"Hope!" cried DeBar. "It's more than hope, man. It's a certainty for me - the end, I mean. Don't you see, Phil - " He came and sat down close to the other on the sledge, and spoke as if he had known him for years. "It's got to be the end for me, and I guess that's what makes me cheerful like. I'm going to tell you about it, if you don't mind."

"I don't mind; I want to hear," said Philip, and he edged a little nearer, until they sat shoulder to shoulder.

"It's got to be the end," repeated DeBar, in a low voice. "If we get out of this, and fight, and you win, it'll be because I'm dead, Phil. D'ye understand? I'll be dead when the fight ends, if you win. That'll be one end."

"But if you win, Bill."

A flash of joy shot into DeBar's eyes.

"Then that'll be the other end," he said more softly still. He pointed to the big Mackenzie hound. "I said he was next to my best friend an earth, Phil. The other - is a girl - who lived back there - when it happened, years and years ago. She's thirty now, and she's stuck to me, and prayed for me, and believed in me for - a'most since we were kids together, an' she's written to me - 'Frank Symmonds' - once a month for ten years. God bless her heart! That is what's kept me alive, and in every letter she's begged me to let her come to me, wherever I was. But - I guess the devil didn't get quite all of me, for I couldn't, 'n' wouldn't. But I've give in now, and we've fixed it up between us. By this time she's on her way to my brothers in South America, and if I win - when we fight - I'm going where she is. And that's the other end, Phil, so you see why I'm happy.

There's sure to be an end of it for me - soon."

He bowed his wild, unshorn head in his mittened hands, and for a time there was silence between them.

Philip broke it, almost in a whisper.

"Why don't you kill me - here - now-while I'm sitting helpless beside you, and you've a knife in your belt?"

DeBar lifted his head slowly and looked with astonishment into his companion's face.

"I'm not a murderer!" he said.

"But you've killed other men," persisted Philip.

"Three, besides those we hung," replied DeBar calmly. "One at Moose Factory, when I tried to help John, and the other two up here. They were like you - hunting me down, and I killed 'em in fair fight. Was that murder? Should I stand by and be shot like an animal just because it's the law that's doing it? Would you?"

He rose without waiting for an answer and felt of the clothes beside the fire.

"Dry enough," he said. "Put 'em on and we'll be hiking."

Philip dressed, and looked at his compass.

"Still north?" he asked. "Chippewayan is south and west."

"North," said DeBar. "I know of a breed who lives on Red Porcupine Creek, which runs into the Slave. If we can find him we'll get grub, and if we don't -"

He laughed openly into the other's face.

"We won't fight," said Philip, understanding him.

"No, we won't fight, but we'll wrap up in the same blankets, and die, with Woonga, there, keeping our backs warm until the last. Eh, Woonga, will you do that?"

He turned cheerily to the dog, and Woonga rose slowly and with unmistakable stiffness of limb, and was fastened in the sledge traces.

They went on through the desolate gloom of afternoon, which in late winter is, above the sixtieth, all but night. Ahead of them there seemed to rise billow upon billow of snow-mountains, which dwarfed themselves into drifted dunes when they approached, and the heaven above them, and the horizon on all sides of them were shut out from their vision by a white mist which was intangible and without substance and yet which rose like a wall before their eyes. It was one chaos of white mingling with another chaos of white, a chaos of white earth smothered and torn by the Arctic wind under a chaos of white sky; and through it all, saplings that one might have twisted and broken over his knee were magnified into giants at a distance of half a hundred paces, and men and dog looked like huge specters moving with bowed heads through a world that was no longer a world of life, but of dead and silent things. And up out of this, after a time, rose DeBar's voice, chanting in tones filled with the savagery of the North, a wild song that was half breed and half French, which the forest men sing in their joy when coming very near to home.

They went on, hour after hour, until day gloom thickened into night, and night drifted upward to give place to gray dawn, plodding steadily north, resting now and then, fighting each mile of the way to the Red Porcupine against the stinging lashes of the Arctic wind. And through it all it was DeBar's voice that rose in encouragement to the dog limping behind him and to the man limping behind the dog - now in song, now in the wild shouting of the sledge-driver, his face thin and gaunt in its starved whiteness, but his eyes alive with a strange fire. And it was DeBar who lifted his mittened hands to the leaden chaos of sky when they came to the frozen streak that was the Red Porcupine, and said, in a voice through which there ran a strange thrill of something deep and mighty, "God in Heaven be praised, this is the end!"

He started into a trot now, and the dog trotted behind him, and behind the dog trotted Philip, wondering, as he had wondered a dozen times before that night, if DeBar were going mad. Five hundred yards down the stream DeBar stopped in his tracks, stared for a moment into the breaking gloom of the shore, and turned to Philip. He spoke in a voice low and trembling, as if overcome for the moment by some strong emotion.

"See - see there!" he whispered. "I've hit it, Philip Steele, and what does it mean? I've come over seventy miles of barren, through night an' storm, an' I've hit Pierre Thoreau's cabin as fair as a shot! Oh, man, man, I couldn't do it once in ten thousand times!" He gripped Philip's arm, and his voice rose in excited triumph. "I tell 'ee, it means that - that God - 'r something - must be with me!"

"With us," said Philip, staring hard.

"With me," replied DeBar so fiercely that the other started involuntarily. "It's a miracle, an omen, and it means that I'm going to win!" His fingers gripped deeper, and he said more gently, "Phil, I've grown to like you, and if you believe in God as we believe in Him up here - if you believe He tells things in the stars, the winds and things like this, if you're afraid of death - take some grub and go back! I mean it, Phil, for if you stay, an' fight, there is going to be but one end. I will kill you!"

CHAPTER XII

THE FIGHT - AND A STRANGE VISITOR

At DeBar's words the blood leaped swiftly through Philip's veins, and he laughed as he flung the outlaw's hand from his arm.

"I'm not afraid of death," he cried angrily. "Don't take me for a child, William DeBar. How long since you found this God of yours?"

He spoke the words half tauntingly, and as soon regretted them, for in a voice that betrayed no anger at the slur DeBar said: "Ever since my mother taught me the first prayer, Phil. I've killed three men and I've helped to hang three others, and still I believe in a God, and I've halt a notion He believes a little bit in me, in spite of the laws made down in Ottawa."

The cabin loomed up amid a shelter of spruce like a black shadow, and when they climbed up the bank to it they found the snow drifted high under the window and against the door.

"He's gone - Pierre, I mean," said DeBar over his shoulder as he kicked the snow away. "He hasn't come back from New Year's at Fort Smith."

The door had no lock or bolt, and they entered. It was yet too dark for them to see distinctly, and DeBar struck a match. On the table was a tin oil lamp, which he lighted. It revealed a neatly kept interior about a dozen feet square, with two bunks, several chairs, a table, and a sheet iron stove behind which was piled a supply of wood. DeBar pointed to a shelf on which were a number of tin boxes, their covers weighted down by chunks of wood.

"Grub!" he said.

And Philip, pointing to the wood, added, "Fire - fire and grub."

There was something in his voice which the other could not fail to understand, and there was an uncomfortable silence as Philip put fuel into the stove and DeBar searched among the food cans.

"Here's bannock and cooked meat - frozen," he said, "and beans."

He placed tins of each on the stove and then sat down beside the roaring fire, which was already beginning to diffuse a heat. He held out his twisted and knotted hands, blue and shaking with cold, and looked up at Philip, who stood opposite him.

He spoke no words, and yet there was something in his eyes which made the latter cry out softly, and with a feeling which he tried to hide: "DeBar, I wish to God it was over!"

"So do I," said DeBar.

He rubbed his hands and twisted them until the knuckles cracked.

"I'm not afraid and I know that you're not, Phil," he went on, with his eyes on the top of the stove, "but I wish it was over, just the same. Somehow I'd a'most rather stay up here another year or two than - kill you."

"Kill me!" exclaimed Philip, the old fire leaping back into

his veins.

DeBar's quiet voice, his extraordinary self-confidence, sent a flush of anger into Philip's face.

"You're talking to me again as if I were a child, DeBar. My instructions were to bring you back, dead or alive - and I'm going to!"

"We won't quarrel about it, Phil," replied the outlaw as quietly as before. "Only I wish it wasn't you I'm going to fight. I'd rather kill half-a-dozen like the others than you."

"I see," said Philip, with a perceptible sneer in his voice. "You're trying to work upon my sympathy so that I will follow your suggestion - and go back. Eh?"

"You'd be a coward if you did that," retorted DeBar quickly. "How are we going to settle it, Phil?"

Philip drew his frozen revolver from its holster and held it over the stove.

"If I wasn't a crack shot, and couldn't center a two-inch bull's-eye three times out of four at thirty paces, I'd say pistols."

"I can't do that," said DeBar unhesitatingly, "but I have hit a wolf twice out of five shots. It'll be a quick, easy way, and we'll settle it with our revolvers. Going to shoot to kill?"

"No, if I can help it. In the excitement a shot may kill, but I want to take you back alive, so I'll wing you once or twice first."

"I always shoot to kill," replied DeBar, without lifting his head. "Any word you'd like to have sent home, Phil?"

In the other's silence DeBar looked up.

"I mean it," he said, in a low earnest voice. "Even from your point of view it might happen, Phil, and you've got friends somewhere. It anything should happen to me you'll find a letter in my pocket. I want you to write to - to her - an' tell her I died in - an accident. Will you?"

"Yes," replied Philip. "As for me, you'll find addresses in my pocket, too. Let's shake!"

Over the stove they gripped hands.

"My eyes hurt," said DeBar. "It's the snow and wind, I guess. Do you mind a little sleep - after we eat? I haven't slept a wink in three days and nights."

"Sleep until you're ready," urged Philip. "I don't want to fight bad eyes."

They ate, mostly in silence, and when the meal was done Philip carefully cleaned his revolver and oiled it with bear grease, which he found in a bottle on the shelf.

DeBar watched him as he wiped his weapon and saw that Philip lubricated each of the five cartridges which he put in the chamber.

Afterward they smoked.

Then DeBar stretched himself out in one of the two bunks, and his heavy breathing soon gave evidence that he was sleeping.

For a time Philip sat beside the stove, his eyes upon the inanimate form of the outlaw. Drowsiness overcame him then, and he rolled into the other bunk. He was awakened several hours later by DeBar, who was filling the stove with wood.

"How's the eyes?" he asked, sitting up.

"Good," said the other. "Glad you're awake. The light will be bad inside of an hour."

He was rubbing and warming his hands, and Philip came to the opposite side of the stove and rubbed and warmed his hands. For some reason he found it difficult to look at DeBar, and he knew that DeBar was not looking at him.

It was the outlaw who broke the suspense.

"I've been outside," he said in a low voice. "There's an open in front of the cabin, just a hundred paces across. It wouldn't be a bad idea for us to stand at opposite sides of the open and at a given signal approach, firing as we want to."

"Couldn't be better," exclaimed Philip briskly, turning to pull his revolver from its holster.

DeBar watched him with tensely anxious eyes as he broke the breech, looked at the shining circle of cartridges, and closed it again.

Without a word he went to the door, opened it, and with his pistol arm trailing at his side, strode off to the right. For a moment Philip stood looking after him, a queer lump in his throat. He would have liked to shake hands, and yet at the same time he was glad that DeBar had gone in this way. He turned to the left - and saw at a glance that the outlaw had given him the best light. DeBar was facing him when he reached his ground.

"Are you ready?" he shouted.

"Ready!" cried Philip.

DeBar ran forward, shoulders hunched low, his pistol arm half extended, and Philip advanced to meet him. At seventy paces, without stopping in his half trot, the outlaw fired, and his bullet passed in a hissing warning three feet over Philip's head.

The latter had planned to hold his fire until he was sure of hitting the outlaw in the arm or shoulder, but a second shot from him, which seemed to Philip almost to nip him in the face, stopped him short, and at fifty paces he returned the fire.

DeBar ducked low and Philip thought that he was hit.

Then with a fierce yell he darted forward, firing as he came.

Again, and still a third time Philip fired, and as DeBar advanced, unhurt, after each shot, a cry of amazement rose to his lips. At forty paces he could nip a four-inch bull's-eye three times out of five, and here he missed a man! At thirty he held an unbeaten record - and at thirty, here in the broad open, he still missed his man!

He had felt the breath of DeBar's fourth shot, and now with one cartridge each the men advanced foot by foot, until DeBar stopped and deliberately aimed at twenty paces. Their pistols rang out in one report, and, standing unhurt, a feeling of horror swept over Philip as he looked at the other. The outlaw's arms fell to his side. His empty pistol dropped to the snow, and for a moment he stood rigid, with his face half turned to the gloomy sky, while a low cry of grief burst from Philip's lips.

In that momentary posture of DeBar he saw, not the effect of a wound only, but the grim, terrible rigidity of death. He dropped his own weapon and ran forward, and in that instant DeBar leaped to meet him with the fierceness of a beast!

It was a terrible bit of play on DeBar's part, and for a moment took Philip off his guard. He stepped aside, and, with the cleverness of a trained boxer, he sent a straight cut to the outlaw's face as he closed in. But the blow lacked force, and he staggered back under the other's weight, boiling with rage at the advantage which DeBar had taken of him.

The outlaw's hands gripped at his throat and his fingers sank into his neck like cords of steel. With a choking gasp he clutched at DeBar's wrists, knowing that another minute - a half-minute of that death clutch would throttle him. He saw the triumph in DeBar's eyes, and with a last supreme effort drew back his arm and sent a terrific short-arm punch into the other's stomach.

The grip at his throat relaxed. A second, a third, and a fourth blow, his arm traveling swiftly in and out, like a piston-rod, and the triumph in DeBar's eyes was replaced by a look of agony. The fingers at his throat loosened still more, and with a sudden movement Philip freed himself and sprang back a step to gather force for the final blow.

The move was fatal. Behind him his heel caught in a snow-smothered log and he pitched backward with DeBar on top of him.

Again the iron fingers burned at his throat. But this time he made no resistance, and after a moment the outlaw rose to his feet and stared down into the white, still face half buried in the snow. Then he gently lifted Philip's head in his arms. There was a crimson blotch in the snow and close to it the black edge of a hidden rock.

As quickly as possible DeBar carried Philip into the cabin and placed him on one of the cots. Then he gathered certain articles of food from Pierre's stock and put them in his pack. He had carried the pack half way to the door when he stopped, dropped his load gently to the floor, and thrust a hand inside his coat pocket. From it he drew forth a letter. It was a woman's letter - and he read it now with bowed lead, a letter of infinite faith, and hope, and love, and when once more he turned toward Philip his face was filled with the flush of a great happiness.

"Mebby you don't just understand, Phil," he whispered, as if the other were listening to him. "I'm going to leave this."

With the stub of a pencil he scribbled a few words at the bottom of the crumpled letter.

He wrote in a crude, awkward hand:

You'd won if it hadn't been for the rock. But I guess mebby that it was God who put the rock there, Phil. While you was asleep I took the bullets out of your cartridges and put in damp-paper, for I didn't want to see any harm done with the guns. I didn't shoot to hit you, and after all, I'm glad it was the rock that hurt you instead of me.

He leaned over the cot to assure himself that Philip's breath was coming steadier and stronger, and then laid the letter on the young man's breast.

Five minutes later he was plodding steadily ahead of his big Mackenzie hound into the peopleless barrens to the south and west.

And still later Philip opened his eyes and saw what DeBar had left for him. He struggled into a sitting posture and read the few lines which the outlaw had written.

"Here's to you, Mr. Felix MacGregor," he chuckled feebly, balancing himself on the edge of the bunk. "You're right. It'll take two men to lay out Mr. William DeBar - if you ever get him at all!"

Three days later, still in the cabin, he raised a hand to his bandaged head with an odd grimace, half of pain, half of laughter.

"You're a good one, you are!" he said to himself, limping back and forth across the narrow space of the cabin. "You've got them all beaten to a rag when it comes to playing the chump, Phil Steele. Here you go up to Big Chief MacGregor, throw out your chest, and say to him, 'I can get that man,' and when the big chief says you can't, you call him a four-ply ignoramus in your mind, and get permission to go after him anyway - just because you're in love. You follow your man up here - four hundred miles or so - and what's the consequence? You lose all hope of finding her, and your 'man' does just what the big chief said he would do, and lays you out - though it wasn't your fault after all. Then you take possession of another man's shack when he isn't at home, eat his grub, nurse a broken head, and wonder why the devil you ever joined the glorious Royal Mounted when you've got money to burn. You're a wise one, you are, Phil Steele - but you've learned something new. You've learned there's never a man so good but there's a better one somewhere - even if he is a man-killer like Mr. William DeBar."

He lighted his pipe and went to the door. For the first time in days the sun was shining in a cold blaze of fire over the southeastern edge of the barrens, which swept away in a limitless waste of snow-dune and rock and stunted scrub among which occasional Indian and half-breed trappers set their dead-falls and poison baits for the northern fox. Sixty miles to the west was Fort Smith. A hundred miles to the south lay the Hudson's Bay Company's post at Chippewayan; a hundred and fifty miles to the south and east was the post at Fond du Lac, and to the north - nothing. A thousand miles or so up there one would have struck the polar sea and the Eskimo, and it was with this thought of the lifelessness and mystery of a dead and empty world that Philip turned his eyes from the sun into the gray desolation that reached from Pierre Thoreau's door to the end of the earth. Far off to the north he saw a black speck moving in the chaos of white. It might have been a fox coming over a snow-dune a rifle-shot away, for distances are elusive where the sky and the earth seem to meet in a cold gray rim about one; or it might have been a musk-ox or a caribou at a greater distance, but the longer he looked the more convinced he became that it was none of these - but a man. It moved slowly, disappeared for a few minutes in one of the dips of the plain, and came into view again much nearer. This time he made out a man, and behind, a sledge and dogs.

James Oliver Curwood

"It's Pierre," he shivered, closing the door and coming back to the stove. "I wonder what the deuce the breed will say when he finds a stranger here and his grub half gone."

After a little he heard the shrill creaking of a sledge on the crust outside and then a man's voice. The sounds stopped close to the cabin and were followed by a knock at the door.

"Come in!" cried Philip, and in the same breath it flashed upon him that it could not be the breed, and that it must be a mighty particular and unusual personage to knock at all.

The door opened and a man came in. He was a little man, and was bundled in a great beaver overcoat and a huge beaver cap that concealed all of his face but his eyes, the tip of his nose, and the frozen end of a beard which stuck out between the laps of his turned-up collar like a horn. For all the world he looked like a diminutive drum-major, and Philip rose speechless, his pipe still in his mouth, as his strange visitor closed the door behind him and approached.

"Beg pardon," said the stranger in a smothered voice, walking as though he were ice to the marrow and afraid of breaking himself. "It's so beastly cold that I have taken the liberty of dropping in to get warm."

"It is cold - beastly cold," replied Philip, emphasizing the word. "It was down to sixty last night. Take off your things."

"Devil of a country - this," shivered the man, unbuttoning his coat. "I'd rather roast of the fever than freeze to death." Philip limped forward to assist him, and the stranger eyed him sharply for a moment.

"Limp not natural," he said quickly, his voice freeing itself at last from the depths of his coat collar. "Bandage a little red, eyes feverish, lips too pale. Sick, or hurt?"

Philip laughed as the little man hopped to the stove and began rubbing his hands.

"Hurt," he said. "If you weren't four hundred miles from nowhere I'd say that you were a doctor."

"So I am," said the other. "Edward Wallace Boffin, M.D., 900 North Wabash Avenue, Chicago."

CHAPTER XIII

THE GREAT LOVE EXPERIMENT

For a full half minute after the other's words Philip stared in astonishment. Then, with a joyful shout, he suddenly reached out his hand across the stove.

"By thunder," he cried, "you're from home!"

"Home!" exclaimed the other. There was a startled note in his voice. "You're - you're a Chicago man?" he asked, staring strangely at Philip and gripping his hand at the same time.

"Ever hear of Steele - Philip Egbert Steele? I'm his son."

"Good Heavens!" drawled the doctor, gazing still harder at him and pinching the ice from his beard, "what are you doing up here?"

"Prodigal son," grinned Philip. "Waiting for the calf to get good and fat. What are you doing?"

"Making a fool of myself," replied the doctor, looking at the top of the stove and rubbing his hands until his fingers snapped.

At the North Pole, if they had met there, Philip would have known him for a professional man. His heavy woolen suit was tailor made. He wore a collar and a fashionable tie. A lodge signet dangled at his watch chain. He was clean-shaven and his blond Van Dyke beard was immaculately trimmed. Everything about him, from the top of his head to the bottom of his laced boots, shouted profession, even in the Arctic snow. He might have gone farther and guessed that he was a physician - a surgeon, perhaps - from his hands, and from the supple manner in which he twisted his long white fingers about one another over the stove. He was a man of about forty, with a thin sensitive face, strong rather than handsome, and remarkable eyes. They were not large, nor far apart, but were like twin dynamos, reflecting the life of the man within. They were the sort of eyes which Philip had always associated with great mental power.

The doctor had now finished rubbing his hands, and, unbuttoning his under coat, he drew a small silver cigarette case from his waistcoat pocket.

"They're not poison," he smiled, opening it and offering the cigarettes to Philip. "I have them made especially for myself." A sound outside the door made him pause with a lighted match between his fingers. "How about dogs and Indian?" he asked. "May they come in?"

Philip began hobbling toward the door.

"So exciting to meet a man from home that I forgot all about 'em," he exclaimed.

With three or four quick steps the doctor overtook him and caught him by the arm.

"Just a moment," he said quickly. "How far is Fort Smith from here?"

"About sixty miles."

"Do you suppose I could get there without - his assistance?"

"If you're willing to bunk here for a few days - yes," said Philip. "I'm going on to Fort Smith myself as soon as I am able to walk."

An expression of deep relief came into the doctor's eyes.

"That's just what I want, Steele," he exclaimed, unfeignedly delighted at Philip's suggestion. "I'm not well, and I require a little rest. Call him in."

No sooner had the Indian entered than to Philip's astonishment the little doctor began talking rapidly to him in Cree. The guide's eyes lighted up intelligently, and at the end he replied with a single word, nodded, and grinned. Philip noticed that as he talked a slight flush gathered in the doctor's smooth cheeks, and that not only by his voice but by the use of his hands as well he seemed anxious to impress upon his listener the importance of what he was saying.

"He'll start back for Chippewayan this afternoon," he explained to Philip a moment later. "The dogs and sledge are mine, and he says that he can make it easily on snow-shoes." Then he lighted his cigarette and added suggestively, "He can't understand English."

The Indian had caught a glimpse of Philip's belt and holster, and now muttered a few low words, as though he were grumbling at the stove. The doctor poised his cigarette midway to his lips and looked quickly across at Philip.

"Possibly you belong to the Northwest Mounted Police," he suggested.

"Yes."

"Heavens," drawled the doctor again, "and you the son of a millionaire banker! What you doing it for?"

"Fun," answered Philip, half laughing. "And I'm not getting it in sugar-coated pellet form either. Doctor. I came up here to get a man, found him, and was gloriously walloped for my trouble. I'm not particularly sorry, either. Rather glad he got away."

"Why?" asked the doctor.

In spite of their short acquaintance Philip began to feel a sort of comradeship for the man opposite him.

"Well," he said hesitatingly, "you see, he was one of those criminals who are made criminals. Some one else was responsible - a case of one man suffering because of another man's sins."

If the doctor had received the thrust of a pin he could not have jumped from his chair with more startling suddenness than he did at Philip's words.

"That's it!" he cried excitedly, beginning to pace back and forth across the cabin floor. "It's more than a theory - it's a truth - that people suffer more because of other people than on account of themselves. We're born to it and we keep it up, inflicting a thousand pricks and a thousand sorrows to gain one selfish end and it isn't once in a hundred times that the boomerang comes home and strikes the right one down. But when it does - when it does, sir -"

As suddenly as he had begun, the doctor stopped, and he laughed a little unnaturally. "Bosh!" he exclaimed. "Let's see that head of yours, Steele. Speaking of pains and pricks reminds me that, being a surgeon, I may be of some assistance to you."

Philip knew that he had checked himself with an effort, and as his new acquaintance began to loosen the bandage he found himself wondering what mysterious mission could have sent a Chicago surgeon up to Fort Smith. The doctor interrupted his thoughts.

"Queer place for a blow," he said briskly. "Nothing serious - slight abrasion - trifle feverish. We'll set you to rights immediately." He bustled to his greatcoat and from one of the deep pockets drew forth a leather medicine case. "Queer place, queer place," he chuckled, returning with a vial in his hand. "Were you running when it happened?"

Philip laughed with him, and by the time the doctor had finished he had given him an account of his affair with DeBar. Not until hours later, when the Cree had left on his return trip and they sat smoking before a roaring fire after supper, did it occur to him how confidential he had become. Seldom had Philip met a man who impressed him as did the little surgeon. He liked him immensely. He felt that he had known him for years instead of hours, and chatted freely of his adventures and asked a thousand questions about home. He found that the doctor was even better acquainted with his home city than himself, and that he knew many people whom he knew, and lived in a fashionable quarter. He was puzzled even as they talked and laughed and smoked their cigarettes and pipes. The doctor said nothing about himself or his personal affairs, and cleverly changed the conversation whenever it threatened to drift in that direction.

It was late when Philip rose from his chair, suggesting that they go to bed. He laughed frankly across into the other's face.

"Boffin - Boffin - Boffin," he mused.

"Strange I've never heard of you down south, Doctor. Now what the deuce can you be doing up here?"

There was a point-blank challenge in his eyes. The doctor leaned a little toward him, as if about to speak, but caught himself. For several moments his keen eyes gazed squarely into Philip's, and when he broke the silence the same nervous flush that Philip had noticed before rose into his cheeks. to go roughing it down in South America. I believe you're honest - on the square."

Philip stared at him in amazement.

"If I didn't," he went on, rubbing his hands again over the stove, "I'd follow your suggestion, and go to bed. As it is, I'm going to tell you why I'm up here, on your word of honor to maintain secrecy. I've got a selfish end in view, for you may be able to assist me. But nothing must go beyond yourself. What do you say to the condition?"

"I will not break your confidence - unless you have murdered some one," laughed Philip, stooping to light a fresh pipe. "In that event you'd better keep quiet, as I'd have to haul you back to headquarters."

He did not see the deepening of the flush in the other's face.

"Good," said the doctor. "Sit down, Steele. I take it for granted that you will help me - if you can. First I suppose I ought to confess that my name is not Boffin, but McGill - Dudley McGill, professor of neurology and diseases of the brain -"

Philip almost dropped his pipe. "Great Scott, and it was you who wrote -" He stopped, staring in amazement.

"Yes, it was I who wrote Freda, if that's what you refer to," finished the doctor. "It caused a little sensation, as you may know, and nearly got me ousted from the college. But it sold up to two hundred thousand copies, so it wasn't a bad turn," he added.

"It was published while I was away," said Philip. "I got a copy in Rio Janeiro, and it haunted me for weeks after I read it. Great Heaven, you can't believe -"

"I did," interrupted the doctor sharply. "I believed everything that I wrote - and more. It was my theory of life." He sprang from his chair and began walking back and forth in his quick, excited way. The flush had gone from his face now and was replaced by a strange paleness. His lips were tense, the fingers of his hands tightly clenched, his voice was quick, sharp, incisive when he spoke.

"It was my theory of life," he repeated almost fiercely, "and that is the beginning of why I am up here. My theory was that there existed no such thing as 'the divine spark of love' between men and women not related by blood, no reaching out of one soul for another - no faith, no purity, no union between man and woman but that could be broken by low passions. My theory was that man and woman were but machines, and that passion, and not the love which we dream and read of, united these machines; and that every machine, whether it was a man or a woman, could be broken and destroyed in a moral sense by some other machine of the opposite sex - if conditions were right. Do you understand me? My theory was destructive of homes, of happiness, of moral purity. It was bad. I argued my point in medical journals, and I wrote a book based on it. But I lacked proof, the actual proof of experience. So I set out to experiment."

He seemed to have forgotten now that Philip was in the room, and went on bitterly, as if arraigning himself for something which he had not yet disclosed.

"It made me a - a - almost a criminal," he continued. "I had no good thoughts for humanity, beyond my small endeavors in my little field of science. I was a machine myself, cold, passionless, caring little for women - thus proving, if I had stopped to consider myself, the unreasonableness of my own theory. Coolly and without a thought of the consequences, I set out to prove myself right. When I think of it now my action appalls me. It was heinous, for the mere proving of my theory meant misery and unhappiness for those who were to prove it to me. I was not cramped for money. So I determined to experiment with six machines - three young men and three young women. I planned that each person should be unconscious of the part he or she was playing, and that each pair should be thrown constantly together - not in society, mind you, for my theory was that conditions must be right.

Through a trusted and highly paid agent I hired my people - the men. Through another, who was a woman, I hired those of the opposite sex. One of the young women was sent to an obscure little place a hundred miles back from the Brazilian coast, ostensibly to act as governess for the children of an American family which did not exist. To this same place, through the other agent, was sent a man, whose duty was to get information about the country for a party of capitalists. Do you begin to understand?"

"Yes, I begin to understand," said Philip.

"This place to which they went was made up of a dozen or so hovels," continued the doctor, resuming his nervous walk. "There was no one there who could talk or understand their language but these two. The consequence - conditions were right. They would be constantly together. They would either prove or disprove my theory that men and women were but machines of passion. I knew that they would stay at this place during the three months I had allotted for my experiment, for I paid them a high price. The girl, when she found no American family, was told to wait until they arrived. The man, of course, had plenty of supposed work to keep him there."

"I understand," repeated Philip.

"The second couple," continued the doctor, forcing himself into a chair opposite Philip, "were in a similar way sent up here - to an obscure northern post which I have reason for not naming. And the third couple went to a feverish district down in Central America."

He rose from his chair again, and Philip was silent while the doctor went to his great-coat and from somewhere within its depths brought out fresh cigarettes. His hand trembled slightly as he lighted one and the flare of the match, playing for an instant on his face, emphasized the nervous tension which he was under.

James Oliver Curwood

"I suppose you think it all very strange - and idiotic," he said, after a few moments. "But we frequently do strange things, and apparently senseless ones, in scientific work. Madmen have made the world's greatness. Our most wonderful inventors, our greatest men of all ages, have in a way been insane - for they have been abnormal, and what is that but a certain form of insanity?"

He looked at Philip through his cigarette smoke as if expecting a reply, but Philip only wet his lips, and remained silent.

"I got six months' leave of absence," he resumed, "and set out to see the results of my experiments. First I went to Rio, and from there to the place where the first couple had gone. As a consequence, five weeks passed between the date of the last letters of my experimenters and the day I joined them. Heavens, man! When I made it known that I wanted them, where do you think they took me?"

He dropped his half-burned cigarette and his voice was husky as he turned on Philip. "Where - where do you think they took me?" he demanded.

"God knows!" exclaimed Philip, tremulously. "Where?"

"To two freshly made graves just outside the village," groaned the doctor. "I learned their story after a little. The girl, finding herself useless there, had begun to teach the little children. I'm - I'm - going to skip quickly over this." His voice broke to a whisper. "She was an angel. The poor half-naked women told me that through my interpreter. The children cried for her when she died. The men had brought flowering trees from miles away to shade her grave - and the other. They had met, as I had planned - the man and the girl, but it didn't turn out - my way. It was a beautiful love, I believe, as pure and sweet as any in the whole world. They say that they made the whole village happy, and that each Sunday the girl and the man would sing to them beautiful songs which they could not understand, but which made even the sick smile with happiness. It was a low, villainous place for a village, half encircled by a swampy river, and the terrible heat of the summer sun brought with it a strange sickness. It was a deadly, fatal sickness, and many died, and always there were the man and the girl, working and singing and striving to do good through all the hours of day and night. What need is there of saying more?" the doctor cried, his voice choking him. "What need to say more - except that the man went first, and that the girl died a week later, and that they were buried side by side under the mangum trees? What need - unless it is to say that I am their murderer?"

"There have been many mistakes made in the name of science," said Philip, clearing his throat. "This was one. Your theory was wrong."

"Yes, it was wrong," said the doctor, more gently. "I saved myself by killing them. My theory died with them, and as fast as I could travel I hurried to that other place in Central America."

A soft glow entered into his eyes now, and he came around the stove and took one of Philip's hands between his own, and looked steadily down into his face, while there came a curious twitching about the muscles of his throat.

"Nothing had happened," he said, barely above a whisper. "I found her, and I thank God for that I loved her, and my theory was doubly shattered, a thousand times cursed. She is my wife, and I am the happiest of men - except for these haunting memories. Before I married her I told her all, and together we have tried to make restitution for my crime, for I shall always deem it such. I found that the man who died was supporting a mother, and that the girl's parents lived on a little mortgaged farm in Michigan. We sent the mother ten thousand dollars, and the parents the same. We have built a little church in the village where they died. The third couple," finished the doctor, dropping Philip's hand, "came up here. When I got back from the south I found that several of my checks had been returned. I wrote letter after letter, but could find no trace of these last of my experimenters. I sent an agent into the North and he returned without news of them. They had never appeared at Fort Smith. And now - I have come up to hunt for them myself. Perhaps, in your future wanderings, you may be of some assistance to me. That is why I have told you this - with the hope that you will help me, if you can."

With a flash of his old, quick coolness the doctor turned to one of Pierre Thoreau's bunks.

"Now," he said, with a strained laugh, "I'll follow your suggestion and go to bed. Goodnight."

CHAPTER XIV

WHAT CAME OF THE GREAT LOVE EXPERIMENT

For an hour after he had gone to bed Philip lay awake thinking of the doctor's story. He dreamed of it when he fell asleep. In a way for which he could not account, the story had a peculiar effect upon him, and developed in him a desire to know the end. He awoke in the morning anxious to resume the subject with McGill, but the doctor disappointed him. During the whole of the day he made no direct reference to his mission in the North, and when Philip once or twice brought him back to the matter he evaded any discussion of it, giving him to understand, without saying so, that the matter was a closed incident between them, only to be reopened when he was able to give some help in the search. The doctor talked freely of his home, of the beauty and the goodness of his wife, and of a third member whom they expected in their little family circle in the spring. They discussed home topics - politics, clubs and sport. The doctor disliked society, though for professional reasons he was compelled to play a small part in it, and in this dislike the two men found themselves on common ground. They became more and more confidential in all ways but one. They passed hours in playing cribbage with a worn pack of Pierre's cards, and the third night sang old college songs which both had nearly forgotten. It was on this evening that they planned to remain one more day in Pierre's cabin and then leave for Fort Smith.

"You have hope - there," said Philip in a casual way, as they were undressing.

"Little hope, but the search will begin from there," replied the doctor. "I have more hope at Chippewayan, where we struck a clew. I sent back my Indian to follow it up."

They went to bed. How long he had slept Philip had no idea, when he was awakened by a slight noise. In a sub-conscious sort of way, with his eyes still closed, he lay without moving and listened. The sound came again, like the soft, cautious tread of feet near him. Still without moving he opened his eyes. The oil lamp which he had put out on retiring was burning low. In its dim light stood the doctor, half dressed, in a tense attitude of listening.

"What's the matter?" asked Philip.

The professor started, and turned toward the stove.

"Nervousness, I guess," he said gloomily. "I was afraid I would awaken you. I've been up three times during the last hour - listening for a voice."

"A voice?"

"Yes, back there in the bunk I could have sworn that I heard it calling somewhere out in the night. But when I get up I can't hear it. I've stood at the door until I'm frozen."

"It's the wind," said Philip. "It has troubled me many times out on the snow plains. I've heard it wail like children crying among the dunes, and again like women screaming, and men shouting. You'd better go to bed."

"Listen!" The doctor stiffened, his white face turned to the door.

"Good Heavens, was that the wind?" he asked after a moment.

Philip had rolled from his bunk and was pulling on his clothes.

"Dress and we'll find out," he advised.

Together they went to the door, opened it, and stepped outside. The sky was thick and heavy, with only a white blur where the moon was smothered. Fifty yards away the gray gloom became opaque. Over the thousand miles of drift to the north there came a faint whistling wind, rising at times in fitful sweeps of flinty snow, and at intervals dying away until it became only a lulling sound. In one of these intervals both men held their breath.

From somewhere out of the night, and yet from nowhere that they could point, there came a human voice.

"Pier-r-r-e Thoreau - Pier-r-r-e Thoreau - Ho, Pierre Thoreau-u-u-u!"

"Off there!" shivered the doctor.

"No - out there!" said Philip.

He raised his own voice in an answering shout, and in response there came again the cry for Pierre Thoreau.

"I'm right!" cried the doctor. "Come!"

He darted away, his greatcoat making a dark blur in the night ahead of Philip, who paused again to shout through the megaphone of his hands. There came no reply. A second and a third time he shouted, and still there was no response.

"Queer," he thought. "What the devil can it mean?"

The doctor had disappeared, and he followed in the direction he had gone. A hundred yards more and he saw the dark blur again, close to the ground. The doctor was bending over a human form stretched out in the snow.

"Just in time," he said to Philip as he came up. Excitement had gone from his voice now. It was cool and professional, and he spoke in a commanding way to his companion. "You're heavier than I, so take him by the shoulders and hold his head well up. I don't believe it's the cold, for his body is warm and comfortable. I feel something wet and thick on his shirt, and it may be blood. So hold his head well up."

Between them they carried him back to the cabin, and with the quick alertness of a man accustomed to every emergency of his profession the doctor stripped off his two coats while Philip looked at the face of the man whom they had placed in his bunk. His own experience had acquainted him with violence and bloodshed, but in spite of that fact he shuddered slightly as he gazed on the unconscious form.

It was that of a young man of splendid physique, with a closely shaven face, short blond hair, and a magnificent pair of shoulders.

Beyond the fact that he knew the face wore no beard he could scarce have told if it were white or black. From chin to hair it was covered with stiffened blood.

The doctor came to his side.

"Looks bad, doesn't he?" he said cheerfully. "Thought it wasn't the cold. Heart beating too fast, pulse too active. Ah - hot water if you please, Philip!"

He loosened the man's coat and shirt, and a few moments later, when Philip brought a towel and a basin of water, he rose from his examination.

"Just in time - as I said before," he exclaimed with satisfaction. "You'd never have heard another 'Pierre Thoreau' out of him, Philip," he went on, speaking the young man's name as it he had been accustomed to doing it for a long time. "Wound on the head - skull sound - loss of blood from over-exertion. We'll have him drinking coffee within an hour if you'll make some."

The doctor rolled up his shirt sleeves and began to wash away the blood.

"A good-looking chap," he said over his shoulder. "Face clean cut, fine mouth, a frontal bone that must have brain behind it, square chin -" He broke off to ask: "What do you suppose happened to him?"

"Haven't got the slightest idea," said Philip, putting the coffee pot on the stove. "A blow, isn't it?"

Philip was turning up the wick of the lamp when a sudden startled cry came from the bedside. Something in it, low and suppressed, made him turn so quickly that by a clumsy twist of his fingers the lamp was extinguished. He lighted it again and faced the doctor. McGill was upon his knees, terribly pale.

"Good Heaven!" he gasped. "What's the matter?"

"Nothing, nothing, Phil - it was he! He let it out of him so unexpectedly that it startled me."

"I thought it was your voice," said Philip.

"No, no, it was his. See, he is returning to consciousness."

The wounded man's eyes opened slowly, and closed again. He heaved a great sigh and stretched out his arms as if about to awaken from a deep slumber. The doctor sprang to his feet.

"We must have ice, Phil - finely chopped ice from the creek down there. Will you take the ax and those two pails and bring back both pails full? No hurry, but we'll need it within an hour."

Philip bundled himself in his coat and went out with the ax and pails.

"Ice!" he muttered to himself. "Now what can he want of ice?"

He dug down through three feet of snow and chopped for half an hour. When he returned to the cabin the wounded man was bolstered up in bed, and the doctor was pacing back and forth across the room, evidently worked to a high pitch of excitement.

"Murder - robbery - outrage! Right under our noses, that's what it was!" he cried. "Pierre Thoreau is dead - killed by the scoundrels who left this man for dead beside him! They set upon them late yesterday afternoon as Pierre and his partner were coming home, intending to kill them for their outfit. The murderers, who are a breed and a white trapper, have probably gone to their shack half a dozen miles up the creek. Now, Mr. Philip Steele, here's a little work for you!"

MacGregor himself had never stirred Philip Steele's blood as did the doctor's unexpected wards, but the two men watching him saw nothing unusual in their effect. He set down his ice and coolly took off his coat, then advanced to the side of the wounded man.

"I'm glad you're better," he said, looking down into the other's strong, pale face. "It was a pretty close shave. Guess you were a little out of your head, weren't you?"

For an instant the man's eyes shifted past Philip to where the doctor was standing.

"Yes - I must have been. He says I was calling for Pierre, and Pierre was dead. I left him ten miles back there in the snow." He closed his eyes with a groan of pain and continued, after a moment, "Pierre and I have been trapping foxes. We were coming back with supplies to last us until late spring when - it happened. The white man's name is Dobson, and there's a breed with him. Their shack is six or seven miles up the creek."

Philip saw the doctor examining a revolver which he had taken from the pocket of his big coat. He came over to the bunkside with it in his hand.

"That's enough, Phil," he said softly. "He must not talk any more for an hour or two or we'll have him in a fever. Get on your coat. I'm going with you."

"I'm going alone," said Phil shortly. "You attend to your patient." He drank a cup of coffee, ate a piece of toasted bannock, and with the first gray breaking of dawn started up the creek on a pair of Pierre's old snow-shoes. The doctor followed him to the creek and watched him until he was out of sight.

The wounded man was sitting on the edge of the cot when McGill reentered the cabin.

His exertion had brought a flush of color back into his face, which lighted up with a smile as the other came through the door.

"It was a close shave, thanks to you," he said, repeating Philip's words.

"Just so," replied the doctor. He had placed a brace of short bulldog revolvers on the table and offered one of them now to his companion.

"The shaving isn't over yet, Falkner."

They ate breakfast, each with a gun beside his tin plate. Now and then the doctor interrupted his meal to go to the door and peer over the broadening vista of the barrens. They had nearly finished when he came back from one of these observations, his lips set a little tighter, a barely perceptible tremor in his voice when he spoke.

"They're coming, Falkner!"

They picked up their revolvers and the doctor buttoned his coat tight up about his neck.

For ten minutes they sat silent and listening.

Not until the crunching beat of snow-shoes came to their ears did the doctor move. Thrusting his weapon into his coat pocket, he went to the door. Falkner followed him, and stood well out of sight when he opened it. Two men and a dog team were crossing the opening. McGill's dogs were fastened under a brush lean-to built against the cabin, and as the rival team of huskies began filling the air with their clamor for a fight, the stranger team halted and one of the two men came forward alone. He stopped with some astonishment before the aristocratic-looking little man waiting for him in Pierre's doorway.

"Is Pierre Thoreau at home?" he demanded.

"I'm a stranger here, so I can not say," replied the doctor, inspecting the questioner with marked coolness. "It is possible, however, that he is - for I picked up a man half dead out in the snow last night, and I'm waiting for him to come back to life. A smooth-faced, blond fellow, with a cut on his head. It may be this Pierre Thoreau."

The words were scarcely out of his mouth when the man kicked off his snow-shoes and with an, excited wave of his arm to his companion with the dogs, almost ran past the doctor.

"It's him - the man I want to see!" he cried in a low voice. "My name's Dobson, of the -"

What more he had meant to say was never finished. Falkner's powerful arms had gripped his head and throat in a vise-like clutch from which no smother of sound escaped, and three or four minutes later, when the second man came through the door, he found his comrade flat on his back, bound and gagged, and the shining muzzles of two short and murderous-looking revolvers leveled at his breast. He was a swarthy breed, scarcely larger than the doctor himself, and his only remonstrance as his hands were fastened behind his back was a brief outburst of very bad and, very excited French which the professor stopped with a threatening flourish of his gun.

"You'll do," he said, standing off to survey his prisoner. "I believe you're harmless enough to have the use of your legs and mouth." With a comic bow the little doctor added, "M'sieur, I'm going to ask you to drive us back to Fort Smith, and if you so much as look the wrong way out of your eyes I'll blow off your head. You and your friend are to answer for the killing of Pierre Thoreau and for the attempted murder of this young man, who will follow us to Fort Smith to testify against you."

It was evident that the half-breed did not understand, and the doctor added a few explanatory words in French. The man on the floor groaned and struggled until he was red in the face.

"Easy, easy," soothed the doctor. "I appreciate the fact that it is pretty tough luck, Dobson, but you'll have to take your medicine. Falkner, if you'll lend a hand in getting me off I won't lose much time in starting for Fort Smith."

It was a strange-looking outfit that set out from Pierre Thoreau's cabin half an hour later. Ahead of the team which had come that morning walked the breed, his left arm bound to his side with a babiche thong. On the sledge behind him lay an inanimate and blanket-wrapped bundle, which was Dobson; and close at the rear of the sledge, stripped of his greatcoat and more than ever like a diminutive drum-major, followed Dudley McGill, professor of neurology and diseases of the brain, with a bulldog revolver in his mittened hand.

From the door Falkner watched them go.

Six hours later Philip returned from the east. Falkner saw him coming up from the creek and went to meet him.

James Oliver Curwood

"I found the cabin, but no one was there," said Philip. "It has been deserted for a long time. No tracks in the snow, everything inside frozen stiff, and what signs I did find were of a woman!"

The muscles of Falkner's face gave a sudden twitch. "A woman!" he exclaimed.

"Yes, a woman," repeated Philip, "and there was a photograph of her on a table in the bedroom. Did this Dobson have a wife?"

Falkner had fallen a step behind him as they entered the cabin.

"A long time ago - a woman was there," he said. "She was a young woman, and - and almost beautiful. But she wasn't his wife."

"She was pretty," replied Philip, "so pretty that I brought her picture along for my collection at home." He looked about for McGill. "Where's the doctor?"

Falkner's face was very white as he explained what had happened during the other's absence.

"He said that he would camp early this afternoon so that you could overtake them," he finished after he had described the capture and the doctor's departure. "The doctor thought you would want to lose no time in getting the prisoners to Fort Smith, and that he could get a good start before night. To-morrow or the next day I am going to follow with the other team. I'd go with you if he hadn't commanded me to remain here and nurse my head for another twenty-four hours."

Philip shrugged his shoulders, and the two had little to say as they ate their dinners. After an hour's rest he prepared a light pack and took up the doctor's trail. Inwardly he rankled at the unusual hand which the little professor was playing in leaving Pierre's cabin with the prisoners, and yet he was confident that

McGill would wait for him. Mile after mile he traveled down the creek. At dusk there was no sign of his new friend. Just before dark he climbed a dead stub at the summit of a high ridge and half a dozen miles of the unbroken barren stretched out before his eyes.

At six o'clock he stopped to cook some tea and warm his meat and bannock. After that he traveled until ten, then built a big fire and gave up the pursuit until morning. At dawn he started again, and not until the forenoon was half gone did he find where the doctor had stopped to camp.

The ashes of his fire were still warm beneath and the snow was trampled hard around them. In the north the clouds were piling up, betokening a storm such as it was not well for a man in Philip's condition of fatigue to face. Already some flavor of the approaching blizzard was carried to him on the wind.

So he hurried on. Fortunately the storm died away after an hour or two of fierce wind. Still he did not come up with McGill, and he camped again for the night, cursing the little professor who was racing on ahead of him. It was noon of the following day when he came in sight of the few log cabins at Fort Smith, situated in a treeless and snow-smothered sweep of the plain on the other side of the Slave. He crossed the river and hurried past the row of buildings that led to post headquarters. In front of the company office were gathered a little crowd of men, women and children. He pushed his way through and stopped at the bottom of the three log steps which led up to the door.

At the top was Professor McGill, coming out. His face was a puzzle. His eyes had in them a stony stare as he gazed down at Philip. Then he descended slowly, like one moving in a dream. "Good Heavens," he said huskily, and only for Philip's ears, "do you know what I've done, Phil?"

"What?" demanded Philip.

The doctor came down to the last step.

"Phil," he whispered, "that fellow we found with a broken head played a nice game on me. He was a criminal, and I've brought back to Fort Smith no less person than the man sent out to arrest him, Corporal Dobson, of the Mounted Police, and his driver, Francois Something-or-Other. Heavens, ain't it funny?"

That same afternoon Corporal Dobson and the half-breed set out again in quest of Falkner, and this time they were accompanied by Pierre Thoreau, who learned for the first time what had happened in his cabin. The doctor disappeared for the rest of the day, but early the next morning he hunted Phil up and took him to a cabin half a mile down the river. A team of powerful dogs, an unusually large sledge, and two Indians were at the door.

"I bought 'em last night," explained the doctor, "and we're going to leave for the south to-day."

"Giving up your hunt?" asked Philip.

"No, it's ended," replied McGill in a matter-of-fact way. "It ended at Pierre Thoreau's cabin. Falkner was the third man to work out my experiment."

Philip stopped in his tracks, and the doctor stopped, and turned toward him.

"But the third -" Philip began.

The little doctor continued to smile.

"There are more things in Heaven and earth, Philip," he quoted, "than are dreamed of in your philosophy. This love experiment has turned out wrongly, as far as preconceived theories are concerned, but when I think of the broader, deeper significance of it all I am - pleased is not the word."

"What I can't see -" Philip was stopped by the doctor's lifted hand.

"You see, I am relying on your word of honor, Phil," he explained, laughing softly at the amazement which he saw in the other's face. "It's all so wonderful that I want you to know the end of it, and how happily it has turned out for me - and the little woman waiting for me back home. It was I and not Falkner who cried out just before you turned the lamp-wick down. A letter had fallen from his coat pocket, and it was one of my letters - sent through my agent. Understand? I sent you for the ice, and while you were gone I told him who I was, and he told me why I had never heard from him, and why he was in Pierre Thoreau's cabin. My agent had sent him north with five hundred dollars as a first payment. To cut a long story short, he got into a card game in Prince Albert - as the best of us do at times - and as a result become mixed up in a quarrel, in which he pretty nearly killed a man. They've been after him ever since, and almost had him when we found him, injured by a blow which he received in an ugly fall earlier in the night. It's the last and total wrecking of my theory."

"But the girl -" urged Philip.

"We're going to see her now, and she will tell you the whole story as she told it to me," said the doctor, as calmly as before. "Ah, but it's wonderful, man - this great, big, human love that fills the world! They two met at Nelson House, as I had planned they should, and four months after that they smashed my theory by being married by a missionary from York Factory. I mean that they smashed the bad part of it, Phil, but all three couples proved the other - that there exist no such things as 'soul affinities,' and that two normal people of opposite sexes, if thrown together under certain environment, will as naturally mate as two birds, and will fight and die for one another afterward, too. There may not be one in ten thousand who believes it, but I do - still. At the last moment the man in Falkner triumphed over his love and he told her what he was, that up until the moment he met her he drank

James Oliver Curwood

and gambled, and that for his shooting a man in Prince Albert he would sooner or later get a term in prison. And she? I tell you that she busted my theory to a frazzle! She loved him, as I now believe every woman in the world is capable of loving, and she married him, and stuck to him through thick and thin, fled with him when he was compelled to run - and her faith in him now is like that of a child in its God. For a time they lived in that cabin above Pierre Thoreau's, and perhaps they wouldn't have been found out if they hadn't come up to Fort Smith for a holiday. Falkner told me that his pursuers would surely stop at Pierre's, and d his wife. By this time he has a good start for the States, and will be there by the time I get his wife down."

Philip had not spoken a word. Almost mechanically he pulled the photograph from his pocket.

"And this -" he said.

The doctor laughed as he took the picture from his hand.

"Is Mrs. William Falkner, Phil. Come in. I'm anxious to have you meet her."

CHAPTER XV

PHILIP'S LAST ASSIGNMENT

Philip, instead of following the doctor, laid a detaining hand upon his arm.

"Wait!" he said.

Something in the seriousness of his manner drew a quick look of apprehension over the other's face.

"I want to talk with you," continued Philip. "Let us walk a little way down the trail."

The doctor eyed him suspiciously as they turned away from the cabin.

"See here, Phil Steele," he said, and there was a hard ring in his voice, "I've had all sorts of confidence in you, and I've told you more, perhaps, than I ought. I don't suppose you have a suspicion that you ought to break it?"

"No, it isn't that," replied Philip, laughing a little uneasily. "I'm glad you got away with Falkner, and so far as I am concerned no one will ever know what has happened. It's I who want to place a little confidence in you now. I am positively at my wits' end, and all over a situation which seems to place you and me in a class by ourselves - sort of brothers in trouble, you know," and he told McGill, briefly, of Isobel, and his search for her.

"I lost them between Lac Bain and Fort Churchill," he finished. "The two sledges separated, one continuing to Churchill, and the other turning into the South. I followed the Churchill sledge - and was wrong. When I came back the snow had covered the other trail."

The little professor stopped suddenly, and squared himself directly in Philip's path.

"You don't say!" he gasped. There was a look of amazement on his face.

"What a wonderfully little world this is, Phil," he added, smiling in a curious way. "What a wonderfully, wonderfully little world it is! It's only a playground, after all, and the funny part of it is that it is not even large enough to play a game of hide-and-seek in, successfully. I've proved that beyond question. And here - you -"

"What?" demanded Philip, puzzled by the other's attitude.

"Well, you see, I went first to Nelson House," said McGill, "and from there up to the Hudson's Bay Company's post in the Cochrane River, hunting for Falkner and this girl - a man and a woman. And at the Cochrane Post a Frenchman told me that there was a strange man and woman up at Lac Bain, and I set off for there. That must have been just about the time you were starting for Churchill, for on the third day up I met a sledge that turned me off the Lac Bain trail to take up the nearer trail to Chippewayan. With this sledge were the two who had been at Lac Bain, Colonel Becker and his daughter."

For a moment Philip could not speak. He caught the other's hand excitedly.

"You - you found where they were going?" he asked, when McGill did not continue.

"Yes. We ate dinner together, and the colonel said they were bound for Nelson House, and that they would probably go from there to Winnipeg. I didn't ask which way they would go."

"From Nelson House it would be by the Saskatchewan and Le Pas trail," cried Philip. He was looking straight over the little doctor's head. "If it wasn't for this damnable DeBar - whom I ought to go after again -"

"Drop DeBar," interrupted McGill quietly. "He's got too big a start of you anyway - so what's the use? Drop 'im. I dropped a whole lot of things when I came up here."

"But the law -"

"Damn the law!" exploded the doctor with unexpected vehemence. "Sometimes I think the world would be just as happy without it."

Their eyes met, sharp and understanding.

"You're a professor in a college," chuckled Philip, his voice trembling again with hope and eagerness. "You ought to know more than I do. What would you do if you were in my place?"

"I'd hustle for a pair of wings and fly," replied the little professor promptly. "Good Lord, Phil - if it was my wife - and I hadn't got her yet - I wouldn't let up until I'd chased her from one end of the earth to the other. What's a little matter of duty compared to that girl hustling toward Winnipeg? Next to my own little girl at home she's the prettiest thing I ever laid my eyes on."

Philip laughed aloud.

"Thanks, McGill. By Heaven, I'll go! When do you start?"

"The dogs are ready, and so is Mrs. William Falkner."

Philip turned about quickly.

"I'll go over and say good-by to the detachment, and get my pack," he said over his shoulder. "I'll be back inside of half an hour."

It was a slow trip down. The snow was beginning to soften in the warmth of the first spring suns by the time they arrived at Lac la Crosse. Two days before they reached the post at Montreal Lake, Philip began to feel the first discomfort of a strange sickness, of which he said nothing. But the sharp eyes of the doctor detected that something was wrong, and before they came to Montreal House he recognized the fever that had begun to burn in Philip's body.

"You've set too fast a pace," he told him. "It's that - and the blow you got when DeBar threw you against the rock. You'll have to lay up for a spell."

In spite of his protestations, the doctor compelled him to go to bed when they arrived at the post. He grew rapidly worse, and for five weeks the doctor and Falkner's wife nursed him through the fever. When they left for the South, late in May, he was still too weak to travel, and it was a month later before he presented himself, pale and haggard, before Inspector MacGregor at Prince Albert. Again disappointment was awaiting him. There had been delay in purchasing his discharge, and he found that he would have to wait until August. MacGregor gave him a three weeks' furlough, and his first move was to go up to Etomami and Le Pas. Colonel Becker and Isobel had been at those places six weeks before. He could find no trace of their having stopped at Prince Albert. He ran down to Winnipeg and spent several days in making inquiries which proved the hopelessness of any longer expecting to find Isobel in Canada. He assured himself that by this time they were probably in London and he made his plans accordingly. His discharge would come to him by the tenth of August, and he would immediately set off for England.

Upon his return to Prince Albert he was detailed to a big prairie stretch of country where there was little to do but wait. On the first day of August he was at Hymers when the Limited plunged down the embankment into Blind Indian River. The first word of it came over the wire from Bleak House Station a little before midnight, while he and the agent were playing cribbage. Pink-cheeked little Gunn, agent, operator, and one-third of the total population of Hymers, had lifted a peg to make a count when his hand stopped in mid-air, and with a gasping break in his voice he sprang to his feet.

The instrument on the little table near the window was clicking frantically. It was Billinger, at Bleak House, crying out for headquarters, clear lines, the right of way. The Transcontinental - engine, tender, baggage car, two coaches and a sleeper, had gone to the devil. Those, in his excitement, where his first words. From fifty to a hundred were dead. Gunn almost swore Billinger's next words to the line. It was not an accident! Human hands had torn up three sections of rail. The same human hands had rolled a two-ton boulder in the right of way. He did not know whether the express car - or what little remained of it - had been robbed or not.

From midnight until two o'clock the lines were hot. A wrecking train was on its way from the east, another from division headquarters to the west. Ceaselessly headquarters demanded new information, and bit by bit the terrible tragedy was told even as the men and women in it died and the few souls from the prairies around Bleak House Station fought to save lives. Then a new word crept in on the wires. It called for Philip Steele at Hymers.

It commanded him in the name of Inspector MacGregor of the Royal Mounted to reach Bleak House Station without delay. What he was to do when he arrived at the scene of the wreck was left to his own judgment. The wire from MacGregor aroused Philip from the stupor of horror into which he had fallen. Gunn's girlish face was as white as a sheet.

"I've got a jigger," he said, "and you can take it. It's forty miles to Bleak House and you can make it in three hours. There won't be a train for six."

Philip scribbled a few words for MacGregor and shoved them into Gunn's nervous hand. While the operator was sending them off he rolled a cigarette, lighted it, and buckled on his revolver belt. Then Gunn hurried him through the door and they lifted the velocipede on the track.

"Wire Billinger I'm coming," called back Philip as Gunn started him off with a running shove.

CHAPTER XVI

A LOCK OF GOLDEN HAIR

As the sun was rising in a burning August glare over the edge of the parched prairie, Philip saw ahead of him the unpainted board shanty that was called Bleak House Station, and a few moments later he saw a man run out into the middle of the track and stare down at him from under the shade of his hands. It was Billinger, his English-red face as white as he had left Gunn's, his shirt in rags, arms bare, and his tremendous blond mustaches crisped and seared by fire. Close to the station, fastened to posts, were two saddlehorses. A mile beyond these things a thin film of smoke clouded the sky. As the jigger stopped Philip jumped from his seat and held out a blistered hand. "I'm Steele - Philip Steele, of the Northwest Mounted."

"And I'm Billinger - agent," said the other.

Philip noticed that the hand that gripped his own was raw and bleeding. "I got your word, and I've received instructions from the department to place myself at your service. My wife is at the key. I've found the trail, and I've got two horses. But there isn't another man who'll leave up there for love o' God or money. It's horrible! Two hours ago you'd 'ave heard their screams from where you're standing - the hurt, I mean. They won't leave the wreck - not a man, and I don't blame 'em."

A pretty, brown-haired young woman had come to the door

James Oliver Curwood

and Billinger ran to her.

"Good-by," he cried, taking her for a moment in his big arms. "Take care of the key!" He turned as quickly to the horses, talking as they mounted. "It was robbery," he said - and they set off at a canter, side by side. "There was two hundred thousand in currency in the express car, and it's gone. I found their trail this morning, going into the North. They're hitting for what we call the Bad Lands over beyond the Coyote, twenty miles from here. I don't suppose there's any time to lose -"

"No," said Philip. "How many are there?"

"Four - mebby more."

Billinger started his horse into a gallop and Philip purposely held his mount behind to look at the other man. The first law of MacGregor's teaching was to study men, and to suspect.

It was the first law of the splendid service of which he was a part - and so he looked hard at Billinger. The Englishman was hatless. His sandy hair was cropped short, and his mustaches floated out like flexible horns from the sides of his face. His shirt was in tatters. In one place it was ripped clean of the shoulder and Philip saw a purplish bruise where the flesh was bare. He knew these for the marks of Billinger's presence at the wreck. Now the man was equipped for other business. A huge "forty-four" hung at his waist, a short carbine swung at his saddle-bow; and there was something in the manner of his riding, in the hunch of his shoulders, and in the vicious sweep of his long mustaches, that satisfied Philip he was a man who could use them. He rode up alongside of him with a new confidence. They were coming to the top of a knoll; at the summit Billinger stopped and pointed down into a hollow a quarter of a mile away.

"It will be a loss of time to go down there," he said, "and it will do no good. See that thing that looks like a big log in the river?

That's the top of the day coach. It went in right side up, and the conductor - who wasn't hurt - says there were twenty people in it. We watched it settle from the shore, and we couldn't do a thing - while they were dying in there like so many caged rats! The other coach burned, and that heap of stuff you see there is what's left of the Pullman and the baggage car. There's twenty-seven dead stretched out along the track, and a good many hurt. Great Heavens, listen to that!"

He shuddered, and Philip shuddered, at the wailing sound of grief and pain that came up to them.

"It'll be a loss of time - to go down," repeated the agent.

"Yes, it would be a loss of time," agreed Philip.

His blood was burning at fever heat when he raised his eyes from the scene below to Billinger's face. Every fighting fiber in his body was tingling for action, and at the responsive glare which he met in Billinger's eyes he thrust his hand half over the space that separated them.

"We'll get 'em, Billinger," he cried. "By God, we'll get 'em!"

There was something ferocious in the crush of the other's hand. The Englishman's teeth gleamed for an instant between his seared mustaches as he heeled his mount into a canter along the back of the ridge. Five minutes later the knoll dipped again into the plain and at the foot of it Billinger stopped his horse for a second and pointed to fresh hoof-marks in the prairie sod. Philip jumped from his horse and examined the ground.

"There are five in the gang, Billinger," he said shortly - "All of them were galloping - but one." He looked up to catch Billinger leaning over the pommel of his saddle staring at something almost directly under his horse's feet.

"What's that?" he demanded. "A handkerchief?"

Philip picked it up - a dainty bit of fine linen, crumpled and sodden by dew, and held it out between the forefinger and thumb of both hands.

"Yes, and a woman's handkerchief. Now what the devil -"

He stopped at the look in Billinger's face as he reached down for the handkerchief. The square jaws of the man were set like steel springs, but Philip noticed that his hand was trembling.

"A woman in the gang," he laughed as Philip mounted.

They started out at a canter, Billinger still holding the bit of linen close under his eyes. After a little he passed it back to Philip who was riding close beside him.

"Something happened last night," he said, looking straight ahead of him, "that I can't understand. I didn't tell my wife. I haven't told any one. But I guess you ought to know. It's interesting, anyway - and has made a wreck of my nerves." He wiped his face with a blackened rag which he drew from his hip pocket. "We were working hard to get out the living, leaving the dead where they were for a time, and I had crawled under the wreck of the sleeper. I was sure that I had heard a cry, and crawled in among the debris, shoving a lantern ahead of me. About where Berth Number Ten should have been, the timbers had telescoped upward, leaving an open space four or five feet high. I was on my hands and knees, bareheaded, and my lantern lighted up things as plain as day. At first I saw nothing, and was listening again for the cry when I felt something soft and light sweeping down over me, and I looked up. Heavens -"

Billinger was mopping his face again, leaving streaks of char-black where the perspiration had started.

"Pinned up there in the mass of twisted steel and broken wood was a woman," he went on. "She was the most beautiful thing I have ever looked upon. Her arms were reaching down to me;

her face was turned a little to one side, but still looking at me - and all but her face and part of her arms was smothered in a mass of red-gold hair that fell down to my shoulders. I could have sworn that she was alive. Her lips were red, and I thought for a moment that she was going to speak to me. I could have sworn, too, that there was color in her face, but it must have been something in the lantern light and the red-gold of her hair, for when I spoke, and then reached up, she was cold."

Billinger shivered and urged his horse into a faster gait.

"I went out and helped with the injured then. I guess it must have been two hours later when I returned to take out her body. But the place where I had seen her was empty. She was gone. At first I thought that some of the others had carried her out, and I looked among the dead and injured. She was not among them. I searched again when day came, with the same result. No one has seen her. She has completely disappeared - and with the exception of my shanty there isn't a house within ten miles of here where she could have been taken. What do you make of it, Steele?"

Philip had listened with tense interest.

"Perhaps you didn't return to the right place," he suggested. "Her body may still be in the wreck."

Billinger glanced toward him with a nervous laugh.

"But it was the right place," he said. "She had evidently not gone to bed, and was dressed. When I returned I found a part of her skirt in the debris above. A heavy tress of her hair had caught around a steel ribbing, and it was cut off! Some one had been there during my absence and had taken the body. I - I'm almost ready to believe that I was mistaken, and that she was alive. I found nothing there, nothing - that could prove her death."

"Is it possible -" began Philip, holding out the handkerchief.

It was not necessary for him to finish. Billinger understood, and nodded his head.

"That's what I'm thinking," he said. "Is it possible? What in God's name would they want of her, unless -"

"Unless she was alive," added Philip. "Unless one or more of the scoundrels searching for valuables in there during the excitement, saw her and carried her off with their other booty. It's up to us, Billinger!"

Billinger had reached inside his shirt, and now he drew forth a small paper parcel.

"I don't know why - but I kept the tress of hair," he said. "See -"

From between his fingers, as he turned toward Philip, there streamed out a long silken tress that shone a marvelous gold in the sun, and in that same instant there fell from Philip's lips a cry such as Billinger had not heard, even from the lips of the wounded; and before he could recover from his astonishment, he had leaned over and snatched the golden tress from him, and sat in his saddle staring at it like a madman.

CHAPTER XVII

THE GIRL IN THE WRECK

In that moment of terrible shock - in the one moment when it seemed to him as though no other woman in the world could have worn that golden tress of hair but Isobel, Philip had stopped his horse, and his face had gone as white as death. With a tremendous effort he recovered himself, and saw Billinger staring at him as though the hot sun had for an instant blinded him of reason. But the lock of hair still rippled and shone before his eyes. Only twice in his life could he remember having seen hair just like this - that peculiar reddish gold that changed its lights with every passing cloud.

He had seen it on Isobel, in the firelight of the camp, at Lac Bain - and he had seen it crowning the beautiful head of the girl back home, the girl of the hyacinth letter. He struggled to calm himself under the questioning gaze of Billinger's eyes. He laughed, wound the hair carefully about his fingers, and put it in his coat pocket.

"You - you have given me a shock," he said, straining to keep his voice even. "I'm glad you had foresight enough to keep the lock of hair, Billinger. At first - I jumped to a conclusion. But there's only one chance in a hundred that I'm right. If I should be right - I know the girl. Do you understand - why it startled me? Now for the chase, Billinger. Lead away!"

Leaning low over their saddles they galloped into the North.

James Oliver Curwood

For a time the trail of the five outlaws was so distinct that they rode at a speed which lathered their horses. Then the short prairie grass, crisp and sun-dried, gave place to a broad sweep of wire grass above which the yellow backs of coyotes were visible as now and then they bobbed up in their quick, short leaps to look over the top of it. In this brown sea all trace of the trail was lost from the saddle and both men dismounted. Foot by foot they followed the faint signs ahead of them, while over their backs the sun rose higher and began to burn with the dry furnace-like heat that had scorched the prairies. So slow was their progress that after a time Billinger straightened himself with a nervous curse. The perspiration was running in dirty streaks down his face. Before he had spoken Philip read the fear that was in his eyes and tried to hide the reflection of it in his own. It was too hot to smoke, but he drew forth a case of cigarettes and offered one to Billinger. The agent accepted one, and both lighted in silence, eying each other over their matches.

"Won't do," said Billinger, spitting on his match before tossing it among the grass. "It's ten miles across this wire-dip, and we won't make it until night - it we make it at all. I've got an idea. You're a better trailer than I am, so you follow this through. I'll ride on and see if I can pick up the trail somewhere in the edge of the clean prairie. What do you say?"

"Good!" said Philip. "I believe you can do it."

Billinger leaped into his saddle and was off at a gallop. Philip was almost eagerly anxious for this opportunity, and scarcely had the other gone when he drew the linen handkerchief and the crumpled lock of hair from his pocket and held them in his hand as he looked after the agent. Then, slowly, he raised the handkerchief to his face. For a full minute he stood with the dainty fabric pressed to his lips and nose. Back there - when he had first held the handkerchief - he thought that he imagined. But now he was sure. Faintly the bit of soiled fabric breathed to him the sweet scent of hyacinth. His eyes shone in an eager bloodshot glare as he watched Billinger disappear over a roll in the prairie a mile away.

"Making a fool of yourself again," he muttered, again winding the golden hair about his fingers. "There are other women in the world who use hyacinth besides her. And there are other women with red-gold hair - and pretty, pretty as Billinger says she was, aren't there?"

He laughed, but there was something uneasy and unnatural in the laugh. In spite of his efforts to argue the absurdity of his thoughts, he could feel that he was trembling in every nerve of his body. And twice - three times he held the handkerchief to his face before he reached the rise in the prairie over which Billinger had disappeared. The agent had been gone an hour when the trail of the outlaws brought him to the knoll. From the top of it Philip looked over the prairie to the North.

A horseman was galloping toward him. He knew that it was Billinger, and stood up in his stirrups so that the other would see him. Half a mile away the agent stopped and Philip could see him signaling frantically with both arms. Five minutes later Philip rode up to him. Billinger's horse was half-winded, and in Billinger's face there were tense lines of excitement.

"There's some one out on the prairie," he called, as Philip reined in. "I couldn't make out a horse, but there's a man in the trail beyond the second ridge. I believe they've stopped to water their horses and feed at a little lake just this side of the rough country."

Billinger had loosened his carbine, and was examining the breech. He glanced anxiously at Philip's empty saddle-straps.

"It'll be long-range shooting, if they've got guns," he said. "Sorry I couldn't find a gun for you."

Philip drew one of his two long-barreled service revolvers and set his lips in a grim and reassuring smile as he followed the bobbing head of a coyote some distance away.

James Oliver Curwood

"We're not considered proficient in the service unless we can make use of these things at two hundred yards, Billinger," he replied, replacing the weapon in its holster. "If it's a running fight I'd rather have 'em than a carbine. If it isn't a running fight we'll come in close."

Philip looked at the agent as they galloped side by side through the long grass, and Billinger looked at him. In the face of each there was something which gave the other assurance. For the first time it struck Philip that his companion was something more than an operator at Bleak House Station. He was a fighter. He was a man of the stamp needed down at Headquarters, and he was bound to tell him so before this affair was over. He was thinking of it when they came to the second ridge.

Five miles to the north and west loomed the black line of the Bad Lands. To a tenderfoot they would not have appeared to be more than a mile distant. Midway in the prairie between there toiled a human figure. Even at that distance Philip and Billinger could see that it was moving, though with a slowness that puzzled them. For several minutes they stood breathing their horses, their eyes glued on the object ahead of them. Twice in a space of a hundred yards it seemed to stumble and fall. The second time that it rose Philip knew that it was standing motionless. Then it disappeared again. He stared until the rolling heat waves of the blistered prairie stung his eyes. The object did not rise. Blinking, he looked at Billinger, and through the sweat and grime of the other's face he saw the question that was on his own lips. Without a word they spurred down the slope, and after a time Billinger swept to the right and Philip to the left, each with his eyes searching the low prairie grass. The agent saw the thing first, still a hundred yards to his right. He was off his horse when Philip whirled at his shout and galloped across to him.

"It's her - the girl I found in the wreck," he said. Something seemed to be choking him. His neck muscles twitched and his long, lean fingers were digging into his own flesh.

In an instant Philip was on his feet. He saw nothing of the girl's face, hidden under a mass of hair in which the sun burned like golden fire. He saw nothing but the crumpled, lifeless form, smothered under the shining mass, and yet in this moment he knew. With a fierce cry he dropped upon his knees and drew away the girl's hair until her lovely face lay revealed to him in terrible pallor and stillness, and as Billinger stood there, tense and staring, he caught that face close to his breast, and began talking to it as though he had gone "Isobel - Isobel - Isobel -" he moaned. "My God, my Isobel -"

He had repeated the name a hundred times, when Billinger, who began to understand, put his hand on Philip's shoulder and gave him his water canteen.

"She's not dead, man," he said, as Philip's red eyes glared up at him. "Here - water."

"My God - it's strange," almost moaned Philip. "Billinger - you understand - she's going to be my wife - if she lives - "

That was all of the story he told, but Billinger knew what those few words meant.

"She's going to live," he said. "See - there's color coming back into her face - she's breathing." He bathed her face in water, and placed the canteen to her lips.

A moment later Philip bent down and kissed her. "Isobel - my sweetheart -" he whispered.

"We must hurry with her to the water hole," said Billinger, laying a sympathetic hand on Philip's shoulder. "It's the sun. Thank God, nothing has happened to her, Steele. It's the sun - this terrible heat -"

He almost pulled Philip to his feet, and when he had mounted Billinger lifted the girl very gently and gave her to him.

James Oliver Curwood

Then, with the agent leading in the trail of the outlaws, they set off at a walk through the sickening sun-glare for the water hole in the edge of the Bad Lands.

CHAPTER XVIII

THE BATTLE IN THE CANYON

Hunched over, with Isobel's head sheltered against his breast, Philip rode a dozen paces behind the agent. It seemed as if the sun had suddenly burst in molten fire upon the back of his neck, and for a time it made him dizzy. His bridle reins hung loosely over the pommel. He made no effort to guide his horse, which followed after Billinger's. It was Billinger who brought him back to himself. The agent waited for them, and when he swung over in one stirrup to look at the girl it was the animal ferocity in his face, and not his words, that aroused Philip.

"She's coming to," he said, straining to keep the tremble out of his voice. "I don't believe she's much hurt. You take this canteen. I'm going ahead."

He gave Philip the water and leaned over again to gaze into the girl's face.

"I don't believe she's much hurt," he repeated in a hoarse, dry whisper. "You can leave her at the water hole just beyond that hill off there - and then you can follow me."

Philip clutched the girl tighter to him as the agent rode off. He saw the first faint flush returning into her cheeks, the reddening of her lips, the gentle tremor of her silken lashes, and forgetful of all else but her, he moaned her name, cried out his love for her, again and again, even as her eyes opened and she stared up into the face of the man who had come to her first at Lac Bain, and who had fought for her there. For a breath or two the wonder of this thing that was happening held her speechless and still lifeless, though her senses were adjusting themselves with lightning swiftness. At first Philip had not seen her open eyes, and he believed that she did not hear the words of love he whispered in her hair. When he raised her face a little from his breast she was looking at him with all the sweet sanity in the world.

A moment there was silence - a silence of even the breath in Philip's body, the beating of his heart. His arms loosened a little. He drew himself up rigid, and the girl lifted her head a trifle, so that their eyes met squarely, and a world of question and understanding passed between them in an instant. As swift as morning glow a flush mounted into Isobel's face, then ebbed as swiftly, and Philip cried: "You were hurt - hurt back there in the wreck. But you're safe now. The train was wrecked by outlaws. We came out after them, and I - I found you - back there on the prairie. You're safe now."

His arms tightened about her again.

"You're all right now," he repeated gently. He was not conscious of the sobbing break in his voice, or of the great, throbbing love that it breathed to her. He tried to speak calmly. "There's nothing wrong - nothing. The heat made you sick. But you're all right now -"

From beyond the hill there came a sound that made him break off with a sudden, quick breath. It was the sharp, stinging report of Billinger's carbine! Once, twice, three times - and then there followed more distant shots!

"He's come up with them!" he cried. The fury of fight, of desire for vengeance, blazed anew in his face. There was pain in the grip of his arm about the girl.

"Do you feel strong - strong enough to ride fast?" he asked.

"There's only one man with me, and there are five of them. It's murder to let him fight it alone!"

"Yes - yes -" whispered the girl, her arms tightening round him. "Ride fast - or put me off. I can follow -"

It was the first time that he had heard her voice since that last evening up at Lac Bain, many months before, and the sound of it thrilled him.

"Hold tight!" he breathed.

Like the wind they swept across the prairie and up the slope of the hill. At the top Philip reined in. Three or four hundred yards distant lay a thick clump of poplar trees and a thousand yards beyond that the first black escarpments of the Bad Lands. In the space between a horseman was galloping fiercely to the west. It was not Billinger. With a quick movement Philip slipped the girl to the ground, and when she sprang a step back, looking up at him in white terror, he had whipped out one of his big service revolvers.

"There's a little lake over there among those trees," he said. "Wait there - until I come back!"

He raced down the slope - not to cut off the flying horseman - but toward the clump of poplars. It was Billinger he was thinking of now. The agent had fired three shots. There had followed other shots, not Billinger's, and after that his carbine had remained silent. Billinger was among the poplars. He was hurt or dead.

A well-worn trail, beaten down by transient rangerss big revolver showing over his horse's ears. A hundred paces and the timber gave place to a sandy dip, in the center of which was the water hole. The dip was not more than an acre in extent. Up to his knees in the hole was Billinger's riderless horse, and a little way up the sand was Billinger, doubled over on his hands and knees beside two black objects that Philip knew were men, stretched out like the dead back at the wreck. Billinger's yellow-mustached face, pallid and twisted with pain, looked over them as Philip galloped across the open and sprang out of his saddle. With a terrible grimace he raised himself to his knees, anticipating the question on Philip's lips.

"Nothing very bad, Steele," he said. "One of the cusses pinked me through the leg, and broke it, I guess. Painful, but not killing. Now look at that!"

He nodded to the two men lying with their faces turned up to the hot glare of the sun. One glance was enough to tell Philip that they were dead, and that it was not Billinger who had killed them. Their bearded faces had stiffened in the first agonies of death. Their breasts were soaked with blood and their arms had been drawn down close to their sides. As he looked the gleam of a metal buckle on the belt of the dead man nearest him, caught Philip's eye. He took a step nearer to examine it and then drew back. This bit of metal told the story - it bore the letters R.N.W.M.P.

"I thought so," he muttered with a slight catch in his voice. "You didn't follow my good advice, Bucky Nome, and now you reap the harvest of your folly. You have paid your debt to M'sieur Janette."

Then Philip turned quickly and looked back at Billinger. In his hand the agent held a paper package, which he had torn open. A second and similar package lay in the sand in front of him.

"Currency!" he gasped. "It's a part of the money stolen from the express car. The two hundred thousand was done up in five packages, and here are two of 'em. Those men were dead when I came, and each had a package lying on his breast. The fellow who pinked me was just leaving the dip!"

He dropped the package and began ripping down his trouser leg with a knife. Philip dropped on his knees beside him, but Billinger motioned him back.

"It's not bleeding bad," he said. "I can fix it alone."

"You're certain, Billinger -"

"Sure!" laughed the agent, though he was biting his lips until they were necked with blood. "There's no need of you wasting time."

For a moment Philip clutched the other's hand.

"We can't understand what this all means, old man - the carrying off of - of Isobel - and the money here, but we'll find out soon!"

"Leave that confounded carbine," exclaimed Billinger, as the other rose to mount. "I did rotten work with it, and the other fellow fixed me with a pistol. That's why I'm not bleeding very much."

The outlaw had disappeared in the black edge of the Bad Lands when Philip dashed up out of the dip into the plain. There was only one break ahead of him, and toward this he urged his horse. In the entrance to the break there was another sandy but waterless dip, and across this trailed the hoof-prints of the outlaws' mounts, two at a walk - one at a gallop. At one time, ages before, the break had been the outlet of a stream pouring itself out between jagged and cavernous walls of rock from the black heart of the upheaved country within. Now the bed of it was strewn with broken trap and masses of boulders, cracked and dried by centuries of blistering sun.

Philip's heart beat a little faster as he urged his horse ahead, and not for an instant did his cocked revolver drop from its guard over the mare's ears. He knew, if he overtook the outlaws in retreat, that there would be a fight, and that it would be three against one. That was what he hoped for. It was an ambush that he dreaded. He realized that if the outlaws stopped and waited for him he would be at a terrible disadvantage. In open fight he was confident His prairie-bred mount took the rough trail at a swift canter, evading the boulders and knife-edged trap in the same guarded manner that she galloped over prairie-dog and badger holes out upon the plain. Twice in the ten minutes that followed their entrance into the chasm Philip saw movement ahead of him, and each time his revolver leaped to it. Once it was a wolf, again the swiftly moving shadow of an eagle sweeping with spread wings between him and the sun. He watched every concealment as he approached and half swung in his saddle in passing, ready to fire.

A quick turn in the creek bed, where the rock walls hugged in close, and his mare planted her forefeet with a suddenness that nearly sent him over her head. Directly in their path, struggling to rise from among the rocks, was a riderless horse. Two hundred yards beyond a man on foot was running swiftly up the chasm, and a pistol shot beyond him two others on horseback had turned and were waiting.

"Lord, if I had Billinger's gun now!" groaned Philip.

At the sound of his voice and the pressure of his heels in her flank the mare vaulted over the animal in their path. The clatter of pursuing hoofs stopped the runner for an instant, and in that same instant Philip halted and rose in his stirrups to fire. As his finger pressed the trigger there came to his ears a thrilling sound from behind him - the sharp galloping beat of steel upon rock! Billinger was coming - Billinger, with his broken leg and his carbine!

He could have shouted for joy as he fired.

Once - twice, and the outlaw was speeding ahead of him again, unhurt. A third shot and the man stumbled among the rocks and disappeared. There was no movement toward retreat on the part of the mounted men, and Philip listened as he slipped in fresh cartridges. His horse was panting; he could hear the excited and joyous tumult of his own heart-but above it all he

heard the steady beat, beat, beat of those approaching hoofs!.
Billinger would be there soon - in time to use his carbine at a
deadly rate, while he got into closer quarters with his revolver.
God bless Billinger - and his broken leg!

He was filled with the craze of fight now and it found vent in a
yell of defiance as he spurred on toward the outlaws. They
were not going to run. They were waiting for him. He caught
the gleam of the hot sun on their revolvers, and saw that they
meant business as they swung a little apart to divide his fire. At
one hundred yards Philip still held his gun at his side; at sixty
he pulled in his mare, flattened along her neck like an Indian,
his pistol arm swinging free between her ears. It was one of the
cleverest fighting tricks of the service, and he made the
movement as the guns of the others leaped before their faces.
Two shots sang over his head, so close that they would have
swept him from the saddle if he had been erect. In another
moment the rockbound chasm echoed with the steady roar of
the three revolvers. In front of the flaming end of his own gun
Philip saw the outlaw on the right pitch forward in his saddle
and fall to the ground. He sent his last shot at the man on the
left and drew his second gun. Before he could fire again his
mare gave a tremendous lunge forward and stumbled upon her
knees, and with a gasp of horror Philip felt the saddle-girth slip
as he swung to free himself.

In the few terrible seconds that followed Philip was conscious
of two things - that death was very near, and that Billinger was
a moment too late. Less than ten paces away the outlaw was
deliberately taking aim at him, while his own pistol arm was
pinned under the weight of his body. For a breath he ceased to
struggle, looking up in frozen calmness at the man whose
finger was already crooked to fire.

When a shot suddenly rang out, it passed through him in a
lightning flash that it was the shot intended for him. But he
saw no movement in the outlaw's arm; no smoke from his
gun. For a moment the man sat rigid and stiff in his saddle.
Then his arm dropped. His revolver fell with a clatter among

James Oliver Curwood

the stones. He slipped sidewise with a low groan and tumbled limp and lifeless almost at Philip's feet.

"Billinger - Billinger -"

The words came in a sob of joy from Philip's lips. Billinger had come in time - just in time!

He struggled so that he could turn his head and look down the chasm. Yes, there was Billinger - a hundred yards away, hunched over his saddle. Billinger, with his broken leg, his magnificent courage, his -

With a wild cry Philip jerked himself free.

Good God, it was not Billinger! It was Isobel! She had slipped from the saddle - he saw her as she tottered a few steps among the rocks and then sank down among them. With his pistol still in his hand he ran back to where Billinger's horse was standing. The girl was crumpled against the side of a boulder, with her head in her arms - and she was crying. In an instant he was beside her, and all that he had ever dreamed of, all that he had ever hoped for, burst from his lips as he caught her and held her close against his breast. Yet he never could have told what he said. Only he knew that her arms were clasped about his neck, and that, as she pressed her face against him, she sobbed over and over again something about the old days at Lac Bain - and that she loved him, loved him! Then his eyes turned up the chasm, and what he saw there made him bend low behind the boulder and brought a strange thrill into his voice.

"You will stay here - a little while," he whispered, running his fingers through her shining hair. There was a tone of gentle command in his words as he placed her against the rock. "I must go back for a few minutes. There is no danger - now."

He stooped and picked up the carbine which had fallen from her hand. There was one cartridge still in the breech.

Replacing his revolver in its holster he rose above the rocks, ready to swing the rifle to his shoulder. Up where the outlaws lay, a man was standing in the trail. He was making no effort to conceal himself, and did not see Philip until he was within fifty paces of him. Even then he did not show surprise. Apparently he was unarmed, and Philip dropped the muzzle of his carbine. The man motioned for him to advance, standing with a spread hand resting on either hip. He was hatless and coatless. His hair was long. His face was covered with a scraggly growth of red beard, too short to hide his sunken cheeks. He might have been a man half starved, and yet there was strength in his bony frame and his eyes were as keen as a serpent's.

"Got in just in time to miss the fun after all," he said coolly. "Queer game, wasn't it? I was ahead of you up as far as the water hole. Saw what happened there."

Philip's hand dropped on the butt of his revolver.

"Who are you?" he asked.

"Me? I'm Blackstone - Jim Blackstone, from over beyond the elbow. I guess everybody for fifty miles round here knows me. And I guess I'm the only one who knows what's happened - and why." He had stepped behind a huge rock that shut out the lower trail from them and Philip followed, his hand still on his revolver.

"They're both dead," added the stranger, signifying with a nod of his head that he meant the outlaws. "One of them was alive when I came up, but I ran my knife between his ribs, and he's dead now."

"The devil!" cried Philip, half drawing his revolver at the ferocious leer in the other's face.

"Wait," exclaimed the man, "and see if I'm not right. The man who was responsible for the wreck back there is my deadliest enemy - has been for years, and now I'm even up with him. And I guess in the eyes of the law I've got the right to it. What do you say?"

"Go on," said Philip.

The snake-like eyes of the man burned with a dull flame and yet he spoke calmly.

"He came out here from England four years ago," he went on. "He was forced to come. Understand? He was such a devil back among his people - half a criminal even then - that he was sent out here on a regular monthly remittance. After that everything went the way of his younger brother. His father married again, and the second year he became even less cut off. He was bad - bad from the start, and he went from bad to worse out here. He gambled, fought, robbed, and became the head of a gang of scoundrels as dangerous as himself. He brooded over what he considered his wrongs until he went a little mad. He lived only to avenge himself. At the first opportunity he was prepared to kill his father and his step-mother. Then, a few weeks ago, he learned that these two were coming to America and that on their way to Vancouver they would pass through Bleak House Station. He went completely mad then, and planned to destroy them, and rob the train. You know how he and his gang did the job. After it was over and they had got the money, he let his gang go on ahead of him while he went back to the wreck of the sleeper. He wanted to make sure that they were dead. Do you see?"

"Yes," said Philip tensely, "go on."

"And when he got there," continued the other, bowing his head as he filled an old briar pipe with tobacco, "he found some one else. It's strange - and you may wonder how I know it all. But it's true. Back in England he had worshipped a young girl. Like the others, she detested him; and yet he loved her and would have died for her. And in the wreck of the sleeper he found her and her father - both dead. He brought her out, and when no one was near carried her through the night to his horse. The knowledge that he had killed her - the only creature in the world that he loved - brought him back to sanity. It filled him with a new desire for vengeance - but vengeance of another kind. To achieve this vengeance he was compelled to leave her dead body miles out on the prairie. Then he hurried to overtake his comrades. As their leader he had kept possession of the money they had taken from the express car. The division was to be made at the water hole. The gang was waiting for him there. The money was divided, and two of the gang rode ahead. The other two were to go in another direction so as to divide the pursuit. The remittance man remained with them, and when the others had gone a distance he killed them both. He was sane now, you understand. He had committed a great crime and he was employing his own method of undoing it. Then he was going back to bury - her."

The man's voice broke. A great sob shook his frame. When he looked up, Philip had drawn his revolver.

"And the remittance man - " he began.

"Is myself - Jim Blackstone - at your service."

The man turned his back to Philip, hunched over, as if bent in grief. For a moment he stood thus. There followed in that same moment the loud report of a pistol, and when Philip leaped to catch his tottering form the glaze of death was in the outlaw's eyes.

"I was going to do this - back there - beside her," he gasped faintly. A shiver ran through him and his head dropped limply forward.

Philip laid him with his face toward a rock and stepped out from his concealment. The girl had heard the pistol shot and was running up the trail.

"What was that?" she asked, when he had hurried to her.

"The last shot, sweetheart," he answered softly, catching her in his arms. "We're going back to Billinger now, and then - home."

Choose from Thousands of 1stWorldLibrary Classics By

A. M. Barnard
Ada Leverson
Adolphus William Ward
Aesop
Agatha Christie
Alexander Aaronsohn
Alexander Kielland
Alexandre Dumas
Alfred Gatty
Alfred Ollivant
Alice Duer Miller
Alice Turner Curtis
Alice Dunbar
Ambrose Bierce
Amelia E. Barr
Amory H. Bradford
Andrew Lang
Andrew McFarland Davis
Andy Adams
Anna Sewell
Annie Besant
Annie Hamilton Donnell
Annie Payson Call
Annonaymous
Anton Chekhov
Arnold Bennett
Arthur Conan Doyle
Arthur M. Winfield
Arthur Ransome
Atticus
B.H. Baden-Powell
B. M. Bower
Baroness Emmuska Orczy
Baroness Orczy
Basil King
Bayard Taylor
Ben Macomber
Bertha Muzzy Bower
Bjornstjerne Bjornson
Booth Tarkington
Boyd Cable
Bram Stoker
C. Collodi
C. E. Orr
C. M. Ingleby
Carolyn Wells
Catherine Parr Traill
Charles A. Eastman
Charles Dickens

Charles Dudley Warner
Charles Farrar Browne
Charles Ives
Charles Kingsley
Charles Klein
Charles Amory Beach
Charles Hanson Towne
Charles Lathrop Pack
Charles Whibley
Charles Willing Beale
Charlotte M. Braeme
Charlotte M. Yonge
Charlotte Perkins Stetson
Clair W. Hayes
Clarence Day Jr.
Clarence E. Mulford
Clemence Housman
Confucius
Cornelis DeWitt Wilcox
Cyril Burleigh
D. H. Lawrence
Daniel Defoe
David Garnett
Dinah Craik
Don Carlos Janes
Donald Keyhoe
Dorothy Kilner
Dougan Clark
Douglas Fairbanks
E. Nesbit
E.P.Roe
E. Phillips Oppenheim
Earl Barnes
Edgar Rice Burroughs
Edith Van Dyne
Edith Wharton
Edward J. O'Biren
Edward S. Ellis
Edwin L. Arnold
Eleanor Atkins
Eliot Gregory
Elizabeth Gaskell
Elizabeth McCracken
Elizabeth Von Arnim
Ellem Key
Emerson Hough
Emilie F. Carlen
Emily Dickinson
Enid Bagnold

Enilor Macartney Lane
Erasmus W. Jones
Ernie Howard Pie
Ethel Turner
Ethel Watts Mumford
Eugenie Foa
Eugene Wood
Eustace Hale Ball
Evelyn Everett-green
Everard Cotes
F. H. Cheley
F. J. Cross
Federick Austin Ogg
Ferdinand Ossendowski
Francis Bacon
Francis Darwin
Frances Hodgson Burnett
Frances Parkinson Keyes
Frank Gee Patchin
Frank Harris
Frank Jewett Mather
Frank L. Packard
Frank V. Webster
Frederic Stewart Isham
Frederick Trevor Hill
Frederick Winslow Taylor
Friedrich Kerst
Friedrich Nietzsche
Fyodor Dostoyevsky
G.A. Henty
G.K. Chesterton
Gabrielle E. Jackson
Garrett P. Serviss
Gaston Leroux
George A. Warren
George Ade
Geroge Bernard Shaw
George Durston
George Ebers
George Eliot
George Gissing
George MacDonald
George Meredith
George Orwell
George Sylvester Viereck
George Tucker
George W. Cable
George Wharton James
Gertrude Atherton

Grace E. King	J. Henri Fabre	Katherine Stokes
Grace Gallatin	J. M. Barrie	L. A. Abbot
Grant Allen	J. Macdonald Oxley	L. T. Meade
Guillermo A. Sherwell	J. S. Fletcher	L. Frank Baum
Gulielma Zollinger	J. S. Knowles	Latta Griswold
Gustav Flaubert	J. Storer Clouston	Laura Lee Hope
H. A. Cody	Jack London	Laurence Housman
H. B. Irving	Jacob Abbott	Lawrence Beasley
H.C. Bailey	James Allen	Leo Tolstoy
H. G. Wells	James Andrews	Leonid Andreyev
H. H. Munro	James Baldwin	Lewis Carroll
H. Irving Hancock	James DeMille	Lewis Sperry Chafer
H. Rider Haggard	James Joyce	Lilian Bell
H. W. C. Davis	James Lane Allen	Lloyd Osbourne
Hamilton Wright Mabie	James Lane Allen	Louis Hughes
Hans Christian Andersen	James Oliver Curwood	Louis Tracy
Harold Avery	James Oppenheim	Louisa May Alcott
Harold McGrath	James Otis	Lucy Fitch Perkins
Harriet Beecher Stowe	James R. Driscoll	Lucy Maud Montgomery
Harry Houidini	Jane Austen	Lydia Miller Middleton
Helent Hunt Jackson	Janet Aldridge	Lyndon Orr
Helen Nicolay	Jens Peter Jacobsen	M. Corvus
Hendrik Conscience	Jerome K. Jerome	M. H. Adams
Hendy David Thoreau	John Burroughs	Margaret E. Sangster
Henri Barbusse	John Cournos	Margaret Vandercook
Henrik Ibsen	John F. Kennedy	Margret Penrose
Henry Adams	John Gay	Maria Edgeworth
Henry Ford	John Glasworthy	Maria Thompson Daviess
Henry Frost	John Habberton	Mariano Azuela
Henry James	John Joy Bell	Marion Polk Angellotti
Henry Jones Ford	John Kendrick Bangs	Mark Overton
Henry Seton Merriman	John Milton	Mark Twain
Henry W Longfellow	John Philip Sousa	Mary Austin
Herbert A. Giles	Jonas Lauritz Idemil Lie	Mary Catherine Crowley
Herbert N. Casson	Jonathan Swift	Mary Cole
Herman Hesse	Joseph A. Altsheler	Mary Hastings Bradley
Homer	Joseph Carey	Mary Roberts Rinehart
Honore De Balzac	Joseph Conrad	Mary Rowlandson
Horace Walpole	Joseph E. Badger Jr	M. Wollstonecraft Shelley
Horatio Alger Jr.	Joseph Hergesheimer	Maud Lindsay
Howard Pyle	Joseph Jacobs	Max Beerbohm
Howard R. Garis	Jules Vernes	Myra Kelly
Hugh Lofting	Julian Hawthrone	Nathaniel Hawthrone
Hugh Walpole	Julie A Lippmann	Nicolo Machiavelli
Humphry Ward	Justin Huntly McCarthy	O. F. Walton
Ian Maclaren	Kakuzo Okakura	Oscar Wilde
Inez Haynes Gillmore	Kenneth Grahame	Owen Johnson
Irving Bacheller	Kenneth McGaffey	P.G. Wodehouse
Israel Abrahams	Kate Langley Bosher	Paul and Mabel Thorne
Ivan Turgenev	Kate Langley Bosher	Paul G. Tomlinson
J.G.Austin	Katherine Cecil Thurston	Paul Severing

Percy Brebner
Peter B. Kyne
Plato
R. Derby Holmes
R. L. Stevenson
R. S. Ball
Rabindranath Tagore
Rahul Alvares
Ralph Bonehill
Ralph Henry Barbour
Ralph Victor
Ralph Waldo Emmerson
Rene Descartes
Rex Beach
Rex E. Beach
Richard Harding Davis
Richard Jefferies
Richard Le Gallienne
Robert Barr
Robert Frost
Robert Gordon Anderson
Robert L. Drake
Robert Lansing
Robert Lynd
Robert Michael Ballantyne
Robert W. Chambers
Rosa Nouchette Carey
Rudyard Kipling
Samuel B. Allison

Samuel Hopkins Adams
Sarah Bernhardt
Sarah C. Hallowell
Selma Lagerlof
Sherwood Anderson
Sigmund Freud
Standish O'Grady
Stanley Weyman
Stella Benson
Stephen Crane
Stewart Edward White
Stijn Streuvels
Swami Abhedananda
Swami Parmananda
T. S. Ackland
T. S. Arthur
The Princess Der Ling
Thomas A. Janvier
Thomas A Kempis
Thomas Anderton
Thomas Bailey Aldrich
Thomas Bulfinch
Thomas De Quincey
Thomas H. Huxley
Thomas Hardy
Thomas More
Thornton W. Burgess
U. S. Grant
Valentine Williams

Various Authors
Vaughan Kester
Victor Appleton
Virginia Woolf
Walter Camp
Walter Scott
Washington Irving
Wilbur Lawton
Wilkie Collins
Willa Cather
Willard F. Baker
William Dean Howells
William le Queux
W. Makepeace Thackeray
William W. Walter
Winston Churchill
Yei Theodora Ozaki
Yogi Ramacharaka
Young E. Allison
Zane Grey